SWEETER THAN CHOCOLATE

SWEETER THAN CHOCOLATE

•

HELEN WINGO

AVALON BOOKS
THOMAS BOUREGY AND COMPANY, INC.
401 LAFAYETTE STREET
NEW YORK, NEW YORK 10003

PRINTED IN THE UNITED STATES OF AMERICA
ON ACID-FREE PAPER
BY HADDON CRAFTSMEN, SCRANTON, PENNSYLVANIA

to
My Granddaughters,
Stephanie, Brie, and Dana Wingo
and
Cassandra, Nicole, and Tracey Tomes,
Who enrich my life

Chapter One

Tracy McMillan tasted a square of toast topped with lobster, inched nearer the glass doors closed to the mild May sea breeze, and carefully assessed the CEO of Winter's Inn.

She hadn't wanted to attend the gala for the re-opening of Winter's Inn, but she couldn't refuse Aunt Charli's request, under the circumstances. Now that she was here, she wanted a good look at the man who planned to chuck Aunt Charli's chocolate shop out of the space it had occupied in the hotel for years.

Clayton Winter stood out in the crowd. He wasn't the only thirtyish, lean, six-foot-tall man in the throng moving between the buffet-laden tables angled across the Hibiscus Room. But the others seemed to fade into the background when he approached.

Maybe his well-cut, dark suit fitted just a little better across his wide shoulders. Or the attentive look in his eyes immobilized his audience when he was engaged in conversation. Or was it his hair, the color of aged mahogany, that brightened in the glow of an ornate crystal chandelier as he moved to join a well-dressed foursome?

Tracy's violet-blue eyes studied him without a tinge of guilt. Even without the distracting physical attributes, the air of confidence practically oozing from every pore would have made him noticeable. As noticeable as the bold signature on the letter Aunt Charli had shown her.

Oh, the letter had been polite enough, but Tracy could read between the lines—pay the rent increase or call a moving company.

She pulled her gaze away as a nearby greeting rose above the subdued clamor in the room. Recognizing the expensive perfume her aunt's friend and fellow shopkeeper used lavishly, Tracy smiled. She turned, setting oversize silver earrings swinging beneath her stylish, chin-length hair, and spoke to a petite woman twice her age. Rose Gaynor, gracefully accepting a champagne glass from a passing waiter, looked nearer thirty-two than fifty-two.

"Mrs. Gaynor. How nice to see you," Tracy returned the greeting affectionately.

The older woman beamed. "I'm glad you're back in Costa Corona. Here to stay?"

"For the weekend." Tracy avoided Rose's look of disapproval. Disappointing Aunt Charli by settling in Taos had disturbed her, too. But she wasn't ready to face old ghosts in Costa Corona. Maybe she'd never be ready. She'd just cruise along, playing at a job and not thinking about responsibility and lasting relationships.

"I had to come to Los Angeles to deliver a painting for the art shop I work for in Taos. So I decided to take advantage of it and spend the weekend with Aunt Charli."

"Art shop." Rose puckered her forehead briefly. "Yes, I remember Charli told me you'd dropped out of business school and gone to Italy to study painting, or something, after your father's death."

Or something, Tracy mused. Dropped out was the operative term. No sixteen-hour days for her. She was convinced that all work and no play had been a major factor in her father's death. It had certainly been the cause of her parents' divorce and her lonely childhood.

She blinked rapidly and locked in on the gist of her companion's words as Rose nodded at the CEO across the room. "We're so glad Clayton Winter came back to Costa Corona. Even though his energy makes me feel old. He's on the move eighteen hours a day, checking on construction, speaking at service clubs, pushing publicity. His whirlwind lifestyle delights Chamber of Commerce members, I'm sure. What's good for Winter's Inn is good for most Costa Corona businesses."

"Another workaholic," Tracy scoffed lightly.

Rose smiled. "We need all the help we can get. Recession hit coast highway shops too."

A pang of guilt pierced Tracy's momentary disdain. For almost two years, she'd been too absorbed in her own despair to consider her aunt's problems. Everything had seemed to go wrong when her father died at forty-six. Even though her parents had been divorced for years, her mother remarked with a note of bitterness that it was the result of his lifestyle. Tracy accepted that. She needed something to blame for the loss of her beloved father.

She'd thrown herself into partying as if she were studying for exams. Instead of healing the pain, her actions deprived her of other relationships. Her fault. She'd cut classes and fought with her fiancé over her new lifestyle. When both he and the college officials threw up their hands in despair, she'd fled to Italy, where her mother and stepfather were living at the time, and stayed on to study art.

Rose placed her empty glass on the tray of a passing waiter. "If my shop depended on tourists, I'd have closed the doors. But, like Charli's Chocolates, Chantilly Rose has enough loyal local customers to break even." She laughed lightly. "I have rainbow-hued daydreams that the reopening of the hotel under Clay's management will boost sales."

Tracy refrained from lifting her gaze heavenward. Not everyone saw a pot of gold at the end of the rainbow. With the shop rents increasing along with the room rates, most renters couldn't see the rainbow for the rain. They were looking for new locations. Except Charli. Optimistically, she hoped for a windfall in the three months before the current lease was up for renewal.

Tracy felt her gaze drawn back to the man causing her aunt concern and, with a look of alarm, saw him threading his way toward her group. She stifled a scowl. She hadn't wanted to meet the CEO until she felt less hostile. He was Aunt Charli's landlord.

Displaying a polite smile, she nodded as Rose introduced her.

''Charli's niece.'' Clay Winter extended a hand and gripped Tracy's fingers firmly. ''I'm happy you could join us this evening.'' Fixing her with his steady gaze, he vanquished every other person in the room to the shadowed sidelines.

Tracy murmured something polite, wishing he would release her hand so the uneasy spread of warmth radiating from his skin to hers would wane. He withdrew his fingers before he withdrew his gaze, and Tracy decided it hadn't been only his touch that caused the unfamiliar rise in her temperature.

She looked toward the balcony overlooking the Pacific Ocean, wishing the breeze ruffling the bougainvillea over the decorative iron railing could penetrate the glass panels to cool her fevered skin. In the background she heard Clay's deep, resonant voice speaking to the older shopkeeper and, for some reason, felt it was directed toward her.

Then another voice joined theirs and Clay turned his head slightly, his attentive look focusing on the newcomer.

It's part of his charm, Tracy thought wryly. The ability to zero in, concentrating on the speaker's words as if he or she were the only person of interest in the room. A flash of disappointment touched her at the realization. He hadn't been interested in her in particular. He gave his attention to any speaker without reservation. The secret of managerial success, no doubt. He certainly had Charli on his side, despite the unspoken threat to evict her. Plus, he was gaining a new convert, from the look of the young man talking to him.

"I'll be in my office at eight Monday morning." The CEO chuckled ruefully. "Eight in the evening, also, most days. If you have any other concerns, come by and discuss them with me." His voice sounded sincere.

Tracy felt a stab of irritation and lowered her eyelashes. Concerns! She had a few concerns she'd like to mention. The increase in the rent of Charli's candy shop, for openers.

Realizing her glare was less than friendly, Tracy lowered her gaze to a cream-topped cracker she'd accepted from a waitress. She doubted if Mr. Workaholic Winter wanted to hear her aunt's problems at eight in the morning—even if she could be here Monday morning. He'd be perusing the newspapers and basking in the glow of praise from the local citizens and shop owners on the renovation of the old hotel.

She felt his gaze on her before he spoke.

"Where's Charli? I haven't seen her this evening. Not still at the shop, I hope." Cheerful concern laced his voice.

"She's at home—a little accident." Tracy didn't elaborate.

His eyes narrowed at her terse reply. "Tell her I missed her." A quizzical look flickered in his eyes before his smile reappeared, then he turned and moved away.

Tracy pursed her lips. So he'd noticed her aunt's absence. At least Aunt Charli would be pleased. She'd insisted, wincing at her bandaged ankle, someone had to represent Charli's Chocolates this evening. After all, the shop had occupied a prime corner of the hotel for over twenty years.

Tracy followed the CEO's progress, noticing his interest was no less intense with the new group. She knew from articles in the newspapers that he was thirty-one, and he looked in superb shape; his workaholic lifestyle hadn't settled in the harsh lines and tired eyes she remembered on her father's face.

A fan of sun lines radiated from the outer corners of clear, hazel eyes, and his lightly tanned skin indicated he didn't spend all his time poring over renovation plans for Winter's Inn. But then, many people conducted business on a sunny southern California golf course, Tracy acknowledged. Her eyes darted away when his head turned toward her for a second. A moment later, she continued her perusal.

Despite his square jawline and wide-set eyes, his face was saved from being too good-looking by a thin, straight nose, she decided. He turned and dipped his head, smiling at a middle-aged woman, and Tracy couldn't help but notice the beautiful shape of his strong mouth. She looked away. She wasn't here to assess the man's attractiveness.

Rose chuckled beside her. "He's as charming as he is handsome."

Tracy grinned weakly, aware of the mischievous glint in the eyes of the petite shopkeeper.

"Don't be embarrassed. A fourth of the women in this room are dressed to attract Clay Winter and another fourth are wishing they looked twenty years younger."

"I can't be accused of that." Tracy tugged her loose, crocheted overblouse lower on the gauzy, gathered skirt that brushed her ankles. It was scarcely sequins and satin, but it was the best she could choose from the meager supply she'd packed for the weekend. Not that she had much sequins-and-satin attire in her closet in Taos. The parties she went to were casual.

"You look lovely." Rose took a sip of golden liquid from a refilled glass. "He is single." She grinned. "But I suppose Charli told you that." She turned her head to gaze across the room. "Can't blame Clay for wanting to restore the family name. This hotel was charming and prestigious when his grandfather managed it. Only, Clay's father had no head for business."

She didn't add, as Tracy had heard someone tell her aunt, that three martini lunches hadn't helped. "He had a stroke a couple of years ago," Rose continued, "but he's doing well now." She also didn't add that a few might call the stroke fortuitous since it brought Clay back to assume management of the inn.

"Clay's accomplished a good deal in the two years he's been here. Did you notice the courtyard is landscaped as it was in his grandfather's day?"

"He hasn't done badly inside either." Tracy cast a glance at the shimmering chandeliers spaced across the ceiling. "As a child, I pretended I was Cinderella dancing with my prince when I was in this room." She grinned sheepishly. "If Aunt Charli knew how many times I sneaked up here, she'd probably still be scolding me."

Rose smiled gently. "I doubt if Charli ever scolded you."

Tracy felt an ache of remembrance and was glad when Rose turned to speak to an approaching guest. How had the good memories become buried beneath an avalanche of bad ones after her father's death? She looked away, toward the wide expanse of sliding glass doors barring the sea air in favor of an electrically cooled climate.

Blinking, she tried to banish the blur in her vision. She'd preferred the old-fashioned French doors that opened to allow the salty sea air freedom to pervade the hallways. Her gaze swung back to the multitude of crystal teardrops shimmering in the light from the candle-shaped bulbs above them. At least Clayton Winter had kept the lovely chandeliers.

The hotel had been erected shortly before World War II, Aunt Charli said, its white stucco walls and strawberry-tiled roof picture-perfect against the backdrop of a midmorning sunlit sea on one side and the rising hills on the other. The elegant, imposing structure had two hundred and forty-something rooms, almost half of them with a dazzling view of sand and sea. On an occasional day, the view extended to Santa Catalina Island.

In past days, the hotel had drawn residents of Pasadena and Los Angeles to spend a summer month or so in the quiet elegance of the sparkling seaside residence. Later, Tracy could recall the bus tour groups and the vacationers and wedding parties.

She didn't remember when the carpets began to look dull and worn and the paint began peeling off the walls. She was only vaguely aware the hotel had fallen on hard times. She'd still thought of it as a castle when she went away to college.

A wave of nostalgia touched Tracy. Even through the fresh paint and powder and glitz, the room was achingly familiar. Almost as if she'd come "home."

In a way, she had. Hadn't she been here more often than in the house her father had paid for by working long days at his law practice? From the time she was six, she'd spent after-school hours at the candy shop with Aunt Charli.

After the divorce, she'd gone to the shop on Saturdays also. She was nine then, and her mother had moved to France with her new husband.

When her father died, the time her parents hadn't spent with her grew in importance. It almost obliterated the small amount of time they had spent together.

Tracy picked up a canapé from the tray of a hovering waiter and turned, as she caught a flash of light, to see the CEO pause for a photographer.

More publicity, she assumed. Charli said press releases and publicity announcements had flooded the tour companies and newspapers, touting the reopening of the once well-known inn. Tracy couldn't fault the CEO on that. A surge of tourists and townspeople coming to see the old hotel would increase Charli's business too.

Though not soon enough to support a rent increase. "Maybe I'll win the lottery and can keep the shop as a hobby," her aunt had teased when Tracy broached the subject. But Tracy had caught the glint of worry before Charli lowered her eyes.

Wiping her fingers on a napkin, she looked for a path through the throng. You'd think Winter would value loyalty when he considered ousting the current shopkeepers. Hadn't Aunt Charli hung in there when the resident occupants of the run-down inn could scarcely afford canned beans, let alone chocolates? She hadn't moved her store to a classier location—

like some of the other shopkeepers had. But for the injured ankle, she'd have been here tonight showing her support.

Tracy realized Rose was speaking to her in time to catch the gist of her question.

"Aunt Charli fell off a ladder," Tracy replied in answer to the query. "Insists she's only turned her ankle and an ice pack will have her walking by morning."

"What was Charli doing on a ladder?"

Another voice from the past echoed in Tracy's ear, and she smiled in recognition as Rose's husband joined them. "Hi, Martin. She was helping a neighbor child rescue a kitten."

"Sounds like Charli. But I'm surprised she's not here, even if she had to come on crutches. She's been looking forward to Clay's reopening party. Her shop is among the oldest on the block and she touts the 'shop locally' motto."

Tracy shook her head in loving acknowledgment. "That shop is Aunt Charli's security blanket." She grinned. "Actually, that's why I'm here. At the party, I mean. After I delivered a painting to a client in Los Angeles, I arrived for a surprise visit just after Aunt Charli fell. She was trying to wrap her ankle in an Ace bandage and she couldn't even stand on it." Tracy grimaced. "Madge came by after she closed the shop, piled half a dozen ice-filled Ziploc plastic bags on Aunt Charli's ankle, and talked her into letting me represent her." Tracy spread her hands. "Without consulting me, of course. So I'm here instead of Aunt Charli on crutches."

"Staying for only a weekend," Rose added, pouting

prettily. "I'd hoped we could get together for dinner one evening. Jolie will want to see you."

"Jolie's here?" Surprise and delight echoed in Tracy's voice.

Rose beamed. "She came early for our twenty-fifth wedding anniversary. We'd hoped you'd come with Charli."

Vaguely, Tracy remembered the invitation. She'd put it aside, planning to send a gift. "I wish I could." Tracy felt her face soften in regret. "Tell Jolie I'll call before I leave." She glanced back at the photo session as Rose's attention turned to an approaching guest.

Clay Winter nodded to the photographer and raised a waiting finger to his night manager as he paused to pose graciously with a group of local businesspeople. But he wasn't thinking about the problem that produced half a dozen creases on his night manager's forehead. Or the publicity for the hotel. Looking past the photographer, his gaze sought the honey-hued blond with the oversize silver earrings whom he'd left near the glass doors.

He smiled for the photographer automatically, his mind on the woman. He'd seen her intense gaze focused on him earlier. When he'd taken her hand, he'd thought her eyes had said she felt it too—the unusual rush of warmth between them at the touch.

Unusual, because he programmed his personal feelings. He liked women, liked to see the reaction on their faces when he gave them his lingering look and slow smile. But they were supposed to react, not he. He couldn't let a serious relationship cloud his thinking. Revitalizing the hotel was a full-time commitment. But Tracy McMillan's wide, violet-blue eyes had bowled him over before he'd had time to get his act together. Which was obvious by the lack of interest she'd displayed. It was the first time he'd struck out so blatantly since grammar school.

He was glad when the photographer asked for a second picture. He'd just located Rose, and a second later, the chin-length hair that looked like it had been brushed with moonlight filled his gaze. Tracy turned her head to speak to Rose's husband, and with the movement her hair parted to reveal delicate earlobes with inch-long silver teardrops that separated into shimmering loops.

His gaze lowered to the lacy tunic covering an underblouse molded closer to her curves. The thin, clingy skirt wasn't visible, but he could still see it in his mind's eye. She was covered from neck to ankle, and yet he found her attire more provocative than the sleeveless, thigh-high dress of the young woman pushing close to him as they posed for the photographer. He saw her lean closer to Rose and Martin and then move away, pausing hesitantly at the impregnable crowd near the door. She looked back at the glass doors.

Tracy moved away from the older group, searching for a way out of the room. People milled around her, pooling, it seemed, at the entrance. With a sigh of resignation, she turned around and made her way to the glass doors. Sliding one open, she stepped onto the balcony and walked to the protective railing.

Moon-fluorescent water flooded her sight, making it difficult to deny a feeling of joy to be back in Costa

Corona. Her lips curved upward in an involuntary smile as she thought about the time she and Jolie had ambled through the inside room, lifting snacks and beverages in their trek.

They'd made it to the balcony, intending to duck behind a gigantic potted ficus to survey their lavish loot, when Aunt Charli spotted them. She'd only winked and said "Don't try those white pinwheel things. It's raw fish," before she turned and went back inside.

Only now did she realize she'd missed her aunt. She'd spent little time with her mother in Italy. Nor had the art classes improved her emotional state. She was no artist. A year studying in Florence had convinced her she might excel in a small craft show. Which wouldn't pay the rent. And the part-time art shop job paid little more.

She did have her college fund, she mused. Not that she meant to return to the university to study business. Her father's heart attack had convinced her overwork was highly undesirable.

She leaned against a bare section of the railing, studying the courtyard below. Hidden ground lights spotlighted red hibiscus plants, bright pink azaleas, and green stalks topped by orange-and-purple bird-of-paradise blooms. Above them, broad banana trees like sea green fans rustled in the breeze. A trickle of laughter floated upward, and Tracy stepped back from the railing.

She grinned suddenly. She was no longer a preteen sneaking up the steps to the castle to daydream, waiting for an unknown prince. She watched a late returning fishing boat wallowing across the distant water, and the memory of Clay Winter's slow smile invaded her thoughts. She tried to brush the image aside.

Clay Winter could never be her prince. She almost giggled at the thought. Romantic interludes laced into his workaholic lifestyle! She couldn't see him climbing a balcony in pursuit of anyone unless it pertained to his work. Well, maybe the scantily clad beauty who had been posing beside him during the photo session, she corrected herself. If the lady was an asset to his career.

On the horizon, the boat moved past her, and she let her gaze follow the moonlit rooster tail rising behind the craft. It seemed the fisherman was putting in as long a day as Clay Winter. She pursed her lips. To each his own.

As for the CEO, he would scarcely be interested in a bohemian lifestyle, and she wasn't interested in a working one. Definitely not a workaholic one.

She heard the glass door open behind her, but she wasn't prepared for the sound of the deep voice that came over her shoulder.

"One of my favorite views." Clay Winter moved beside her and gazed across the expanse to the silver-streaked sea. "I use to sneak up here when I was a teenager and eat lunch on the patio if there was no meeting going on in the Hibiscus Room."

"You used to come to the hotel?" Tracy asked.

He nodded.

"Why didn't I ever see you?" she said lightly. "I spent every afternoon after school around Aunt Charli's shop." She cast a quick look at Clay's face, knowing she wouldn't have forgotten it, even if she had been an "uninterested in boys" preteen. "I think I'd have remembered you."

"If I'd seen that perky nose passing me, I'd certainly remember." He grinned mischievously. "So where were you when I spent a month here every summer with my dad after my parents divorced?"

"Summer." She rolled her eyes upward. "That's when I learned to be a camper. If my mother and stepfather were traveling, Dad packed me off to a camp in the mountains."

"Fate," Clay moaned humorously. "But now that we've finally got together, we have a lot of lost time to make up for." Gazing into her eyes, he raised a hand to shield her cheek from a delicate spray of bougainvillea swept upward by the breeze. "Shall we start with dinner tomorrow evening?"

Tracy felt a pulse beat in the hollow of her throat. "I have an engagement." The words sounded like she'd been running.

"Sunday, then?"

Tracy let her gaze drift seaward, noting the boat had chugged out of sight, leaving only the fading trail of moonlight on the water. A breeze ruffled the banana leaves again, spreading fragrance from mimosa blossoms across the balcony, and she thought fleetingly of delaying her departure until Monday. Maybe they could discuss Aunt Charli's lease. An inner voice refused to allow her to pursue the thought. "I plan to return to Taos Sunday."

"So soon?" Disappointment edged Clay's voice. "But you will be returning to visit Charli, so I'm putting in a bid for dinner then."

"Is persistence part of your management program?"

"It helps."

"I won't have any vacation time for six months."

"Holidays? Long weekends?" The slow smile was paralyzing. "Now that we've found we have something common in our pasts, I think we need to compare notes."

Tracy lowered her gaze to the first button on his jacket. Why was she surprised that he was working even when he sounded like he was playing? She should have known the CEO's interest in her had to be related to financial benefits to the hotel. She felt a twinge of guilt. But hadn't she, too, had a fleeting thought of discussing her aunt's lease while idling over dinner?

"Maybe I can remember something about the hotel that you can use in the publicity releases," she said wryly.

A cloud hovered over the mischievous hazel eyes. "Nostalgia sells." He kept a note of humor in his voice.

"I've seen the newspaper articles chronicling the historical data about the hotel. It is interesting."

"I suggest we update the data." The CEO's humorous tone was as unbusinesslike as the sparkle in his eyes.

Confused by the unusual warmth spreading through her, Tracy caught a breeze-swept vine as if it was an anchor and slowly wove it back amid the bougainvillea plant. "I really must say good night." She was relieved to find the turmoil in her mind hadn't affected her voice. "I want to see Aunt Charli before she goes to sleep."

Well aware that Clay Winter's look followed her, she concentrated on spacing her steps calmly across the balcony. She didn't take a deep breath until she paused in the spacious lobby of the hotel.

Leaving Sunday as planned was a wise decision. She nodded to herself unconsciously and then looked up to see if anyone had noticed. The occupants of the lobby seemed absorbed in their own endeavors.

Tracy smiled brightly at an uninterested audience and hurried past an exotic bird-of-paradise arrangement in a two-foot vase topping an antique round table. She paused near a large collector's case as if the variety of seashells on the lighted shelves couldn't be ignored.

Stepping closer, she concentrated on attaching a name to each familiar shell while her breathing slowed. She started with the columbellas and conch shells, frowned a little at the chestnut cowries, and easily remembered the scallops, clams, abalone. By the time she'd reached the turbans, bonnets, and helmets her breathing was normal.

Her equilibrium restored, she strolled out of the hotel, determinedly ignoring the small inner voice that questioned her decision to dash back to Taos.

Chapter Two

Tracy pressed the remote control button beside the door to the back entry and glanced at her watch, waiting for the garage door to lower behind her aunt's small station wagon. The hands on the silver watch moved toward eleven o'clock. Tracy opened the door to the service room and paced across the lighted kitchen, expecting to hear the blare of late news from the television set. Light flowed over the Formica counters, and a strong odor of coffee wafted from a coffeemaker sporting a red light indicating the unit was still on. Tracy wrinkled her nose and crossed to flip the switch to off. Aunt Charli must be sound asleep in her lounger not to be bothered by the foul odor of overdone coffee.

Tracy bypassed the more formal living room to go to the comfortably furnished den. She found the television screen dark and the lounge chairs empty of inhabitants. Scowling, she wondered if Madge had helped Aunt Charli to her bedroom upstairs and then gone home. She glanced toward the staircase. Madge had assured her she'd stay with Aunt Charli until Tracy got back to the town house.

She found the note on the refrigerator when she came downstairs again. Madge's barely decipherable handwriting said she'd convinced Charli to go to the hospital emergency room when the pain in her ankle had increased.

The emergency room. Tracy caught her breath. Aunt Charli had insisted it was only a sprained ankle. By the time she'd taken another breath she told herself it might still be a sprained ankle, but doctors didn't make house calls or open their offices at midnight for minor injuries. Of course, Aunt Charli would have had to go to the emergency room for pain medication.

Punching the remote control button again, she closed the inner door to the house and hurried around the station wagon. She was backing out when it occurred to her she should have called the hospital first. They might already be on their way home. Madge hadn't noted a time in her scribbled note. Halfway to the nearby hospital, she had another thought. Madge might have taken her aunt to the larger hospital in Newport Beach.

Forcing herself to calm down, Tracy drove to the small community hospital and parked in a lot near the emergency room sign. She was three steps inside the entry when Madge hailed her.

"I see you found my note." The middle-aged woman pushed a tangle of curly, gray-streaked hair back from her forehead. "Charli wouldn't let me call you at the hotel."

"Has a doctor examined Aunt Charli yet? Is she okay?"

"She's still in the emergency room, but I think you can go and see her." She motioned for Tracy to follow her, bypassing a clerk who looked at them quizzically.

Aunt Charli lay on a narrow gurney, her head raised six or more inches, and grinned wryly at Tracy as she entered the cubicle. Her aunt didn't look critical, Tracy thought, taking a breath. Not a hair of Charli's heavily sprayed hair was out of place. Tinted reddish-blond this month, it was as rosy as her flushed cheeks and slightly less colorful than the lipstick that Tracy could bet had been applied before Charli came to the hospital.

A young man who looked more like a college football player than a doctor lowered an X ray and nodded to Tracy before he turned to his patient. "I think we'll have to keep you overnight."

Charli moaned and made a face. "I have to open the shop in the morning."

"As if I don't know how to open the shop after ten years!" Madge teased.

Charli grinned weakly. "I know. That was the easiest protest I could come up with." She looked at the doctor with a pained grin. "I can't afford to stay in the hospital."

He gave her a sympathetic smile. "Can anyone 'afford' to stay in hospitals these days?"

"You can probably afford it more than I can," Charli said with a mournful grin, "if your insurance hasn't been canceled."

Tracy frowned. Another problem Aunt Charli hadn't mentioned. She pressed her aunt's hand.

The doctor pursed his lips in further sympathy. "Stabilizing the ankle with a steel pin seems necessary in your case. Pinning the ankle means you'll need a little anesthetic and a short session in the operating room." The doctor smiled briefly as if the sympathy session was out of the way and it was time to get on with the problem. "The anesthesiologist will want to see the results of a few tests before he puts you to sleep." He patted her hand. "Nothing frightening . . . a chest X ray, an electrocardiogram, and a blood sample."

Charli gave another moan.

The physician shifted the X ray to his left hand. "The tests are necessary before surgery. And stop counting costs before you get the bill. I'm sure you can work out something with the hospital."

Charli remained silent, lifting her gaze heavenward. She looked down again when a nurse approached unfolding a hospital gown. She eyed it with a resigned look. "If I'm going to pay spa rates, couldn't I have a designer gown?"

"I'll put that idea in the suggestion box," the nurse said cheerfully. "Meanwhile, if you'll make do with this, I'll add a few of our 'hero,' 'heroine,' and 'happy face' stickers."

Charli smiled weakly. "I'm not usually this grumpy."

Madge touched her employer's arm, concern evident in her eyes. "With an autographed cast and a decorated gown, you'll be the hit of the hospital dress parade.'' Her teasing tone concealed her anxiety. "I don't see why you have a long face. Trade places. You slave over melting chocolate—I could stand the rest, not to mention the TLC.''

Charli wrinkled her nose at Madge, then looked solemn. "I'm afraid you'll even have to give up your day off this week, ole friend. But I'll make it up to you.''

"You always do. Now stop worrying,'' Madge said briskly. "I imagine the nurse is waiting for us to leave so she can poke you with needles or take your blood pressure or something.''

The nurse smiled, looking first at Madge and then at Tracy. "If one of you will give the admitting clerk the rest of the information for Mrs. Nieblas, I'll help her with the gown and then take her upstairs. Room two-sixteen, if you want to come and say good night later.'' She pulled aside the enclosing curtain for Madge and Tracy to leave.

Tracy released her aunt's hand reluctantly. "I'll be up to see you in a few minutes, Aunt Charli.'' She stepped away from the gurney and walked outside the curtain to join Madge.

"When did Aunt Charli's insurance lapse?'' Tracy asked.

Madge rolled her eyes upward. "Months ago. She's been trying to cut expenses and she said she hadn't been sick in twenty years.'' Madge drew her thin lips and shook her head. "She kept up the payments on employee insurance.''

Tracy frowned and walked to the admitting desk.

A secretary smiled at them brightly. "Are you relatives of . . .'' She hesitated and looked at a form on the desk. "Mrs. Nieblas?''

Tracy nodded. "She's my aunt."

The secretary punched a letter on the keyboard located in front of the computer monitor and looked at the blue screen expectantly. Fingers poised over the keys as if awaiting a start signal, she cleared her throat. Without looking at Tracy, she typed information as Tracy answered her questions. She looked up when she seemed satisfied with the data on the screen. "Would you happen to have your aunt's insurance card or forms with you?" She looked at Tracy solemnly.

Tracy clenched the straps of her shoulder bag with a fleeting panic. Would they refuse to admit Aunt Charli if she had no insurance?

"No." She took a deep breath. "Could I check with Aunt Charli tomorrow?"

The clerk's fingers flexed over the keyboard.

"Aunt Charli is the proprietor of the chocolate shop in Winter's Inn."

The clerk's expression didn't change. "Tomorrow will be fine."

Tracy withheld a sigh of relief and wondered if Aunt Charli had any money in a savings account.

She didn't mention money when she went to say good night to her aunt. Nor did she mention it when she parted with Madge. But she could think of nothing else when she tossed and turned in the bed of Aunt Charli's guest room.

Clay opened the drapes of the room he'd used when he visited his father in earlier years. The furniture had been changed from shelves for his model car collection and bunk beds for his sleepover friends to more sedate twin beds and bureaus.

He breathed deeply, filling his lungs with the tangy air, and filled his sight with the view highlighted by the brilliant morning sun. A lone gardener raked the expanse of grass stretching toward the staircase leading to the water below the broad, two-story house. On the water, gentle waves curled into lace-edged rolls that unfolded again, sliding smoothly onward to caress the gilded sand. Clay turned away from the window. Too late for his morning jog on the beach, he decided.

He'd arrived home well after two last night, then his sleep had been interrupted with thoughts of the violet-eyed beauty related to Charli. He'd been attracted to Tracy McMillan the minute he'd seen the laughter in the unusual eyes. Touching her had only increased the attraction. For a moment, he'd thought she felt the same attraction. Then she'd pulled her hand away and her feelings with it.

He took a pair of gray trousers from the closet, telling himself to forget her. She would only be around for a day. Besides, he had little time for activities not directly concerned with the hotel. He pulled on the trousers and reached for a pale blue shirt. Slinging a navy jacket over his arm, he took the stairs two at a time and went to the kitchen.

He eyed the leftover coffee in the glass carafe with distaste. Lifting the carafe, he emptied the contents into the sink. He'd have coffee at the hotel with his father before he went to his office. Clement Winter should be up by this time.

He didn't mind that his father wanted to live at the hotel. The stroke had left him faintly forgetful. And if he found security in the familiar corridors of the hotel and the familiar faces of longtime employees, Clay was grateful.

The older man didn't involve himself with the renovation plans or the running of the hotel. But then, Clement had never let hotel problems take up too much of his time. Managing Winter's Inn had long been Clay's dream. And restoring it to the splendor of his grandfather's day had become almost an obsession.

But behind his passion was an unspoken love for his father. The dreamy, dazed state his father had lived in most of his adult life was overpowered by the memory of the times his father had left the office to go on an outing with him. He'd looked forward to holidays and one summer month in California every year. Only when he became older did the alcoholic haze clouding his father's mind upset him.

He surmised he'd inherited his workaholism from his grandfather or developed it through the efforts of his mother, who'd abhorred his father's idleness reinforced by his drinking. She'd divorced Clement before the hotel started going downhill, but she often pointed out her former husband's weaknesses and failures as a warning to Clay.

Then his father had suffered a stroke, and Clay had covered the unpleasant reality of the hotel's near demise with the memory of the times spent with his father.

He told himself he wanted to return the hotel to its former elegance. And it was true. Only, unspoken was the need to succeed for his father. The hotel was Clement's real home. Clay wanted it open and thriving, with a room available for his father.

Even though Clement Winter had not had a drink for over two years, Clay found he still wore his familiar, slightly dazed smile when he opened the door. The elder Winter was dressed in a light sports coat and fawn-colored trousers, and the neck of his cream-colored shirt was open, revealing a gold chain.

"Good morning, Clay," he greeted his son cheerfully. "You're just in time to have breakfast with me."

"That's why I came early. But I'll just order coffee for myself." He walked toward the telephone.

"Let's not stay in the room." Clement held the door open.

"Your balcony has the best view of the ocean in the hotel."

"But I've seen it," Clement said jovially. "Let's go to the parade."

Clay replaced the receiver. *Go to the parade.* Familiar words from his childhood. He'd been ten or eleven the first time he'd heard them. His father had told his secretary he had an appointment, winked at his waiting son when they were out of sight, and uttered the familiar words. The parade proved to be a trip to Disneyland that day. But trips to museums, art galleries, and amusement parks, or just sitting on a bench watching people stroll by, also qualified. Work didn't.

Grinning, Clay followed his father into the hall, quelling the impulse to rush to his office. It was Saturday, he reminded himself. He had no appointments, and the print on the stack of paperwork on his desk wouldn't fade in an hour.

Turning the corner after leaving the elevator, Clay

stopped short, an unexpected rush of pleasure touching him. Tracy McMillan strode across the lobby, evidently headed for the restaurant. Another early riser who hadn't stopped for coffee. She halted at the sound of his voice speaking her name, and her violet-blue eyes met his. For a second, he felt tongue-tied.

"Morning." His voice emerged in a well-modulated tone, to his surprise.

Tracy nodded, her gaze shifting to Clay's father. "Good morning, Mr. Winter. I hoped I'd see you while I was in town. Tracy McMillan, Charli's niece," she added, giving him no chance to question his memory.

Clement tipped his head graciously and smiled his familiar smile. "As if I could forget." He held forth a pale hand and clasped Tracy's fingers. Releasing his frail grip, he turned to Clay. "You do remember Tracy, don't you? She was here often enough when she was younger." His eyes softened in reflection. "She once asked me if the hotel was my castle. I probably said yes. The place wasn't a burden when I first took over the management from my father."

Clay's gaze sharpened. He'd never heard his father complain about the problems at the hotel.

Clement looked away then, his eyes misting, and Clay looked hurriedly at Tracy, but she was loosening the clasp on her handbag.

"Didn't expect to see you here so early," he said with a rush of cheerfulness.

Tracy grinned weakly, wondering if the amount of caffeine she'd consumed in the hospital waiting room was responsible for the acceleration in her heart rate.

"Thought I'd stop for a little toast to soak up some of the burnt coffee I've been drinking this morning."

"Burnt coffee here?" Clay raised an eyebrow.

"No, at the hospital."

"What have you been doing at the hospital?" He blinked and answered his own question. "Charli. Charli must have had more than a little accident."

"The sprained ankle turned out to be broken in a couple of places." Tracy grimaced.

"Pretty serious?" Concern touched Clay's voice.

"Serious enough to have a steel pin inserted to anchor it, or something like that. Aunt Charli was scheduled for surgery this morning, but an emergency C-section had priority. So she insisted I come down to see if Madge had opened the shop. Said Madge might need to send me for change or something." Tracy rolled her eyes. "I think she wanted me to stop fussing over her."

"Tracy." The faintest lisp tainted Clement Winter's voice. "We're on our way to breakfast. Will you join us?"

Tracy glanced toward the restaurant. "I'd planned to grab some toast and fruit in the café."

A flash of disappointment touched the older man's eyes. "I thought we might eat on the patio of the Shell Room. Sun and sea and the smell of honeysuckle blossoms."

Tracy felt a flush of guilt. How could she refuse? Clement Winter had been as kind and courteous to her as his given name signified, when she was younger. She withheld a sigh and smiled, noting when her look met his eyes that they were unusually clear. His hair, too, had changed. The once rich, brown mane was white, gloriously white. It had been cut well and brushed carefully to spread the thinning locks over his head. Soft, pale, slightly plump skin had replaced the once taut, suntanned cheeks she remembered. The dignity with which he'd always walked was slightly marred by what was apparently a weakened leg. Only the charming smile was the same.

"I can order toast and fruit on the Shell Room patio," Tracy said, returning the broad smile. "Thank you for asking me. I love the smell of honeysuckle and salt air." Warmth encircled her as she was rewarded with a look of pleasure from Clement. She felt even warmer when she saw the look in Clay's eyes. It was a mixture of both gratitude and admiration— and something she wasn't sure she wanted to attach a name to.

Glancing at Clay as they progressed across the lobby, she was pleasantly surprised. For a type A personality, he exhibited extraordinary patience with his father's slow progress across the room. Not one wrinkle of irritation creased his mouth when Clement stopped to speak to a silver-haired senior citizen. Then she noticed Clay using the time to scan the lobby, checking on the actions of the bellboys and the admitting desk clerks. His eyes seemed to be gathering data to store in his mental computer.

A white-jacketed waiter approached, carrying a coffee carafe, by the time Tracy had settled in her chair.

Clement watched as the liquid filled the cups, then lifted his coffee carefully with his left hand, leaving his right hand resting below the table. "I suppose you'll be staying to help in the shop now," he said.

Tracy stared at him for a moment and then blinked.

She'd deliberately refused to think past giving Aunt Charli the rest of her college fund to pay the hospital bill. Hadn't the doctor said she would be out of the hospital in a day or two? A broken ankle wasn't serious. Aunt Charli would laugh at the idea that she needed any help. She'd probably open the shop herself on Tuesday or Wednesday.

"I have a job in New Mexico," Tracy said hesitantly. "I'm due back Monday." She paused as a waiter placed toast and fresh fruit before her. First Rose and now Clement, expecting her to stay in Costa Corona. Maybe Aunt Charli didn't want any help. Had they thought of that? The waiter moved away and Tracy looked at Clement. "I plan to call my boss and ask for a few more days off. Until Aunt Charli gets home from the hospital." Tracy sensed Clement's relief as he smiled, nodded, and poked his fork carefully at the blueberry waffles in front of him. At least she had him off her back. She looked aside, noting Clay signal a waiter.

"Are you ready for a refill?" He nodded at Tracy's half-full cup.

Anxious to back away from any conversation about staying in the shop, Tracy nodded and scanned the patio dining area. "Breakfast business looks good," she said lightly. "I hope this is a sign of more to come."

"It's a start," Clay said. He thanked the waiter and turned back to Tracy. "We have a few conferences booked, and the tourist season is coming up. We have two local clubs signed up for their weekly luncheon meetings, three wedding receptions, and one anniversary party that I know of."

"I hope your guests find their way to the chocolate shop. Aunt Charli could use the revenue."

"I'll point everyone I meet on the premises in that direction." His smile spread like the generous dollop of strawberry jam he smoothed on a piece of whole-wheat toast. "I want my renters to be happy."

Clement laughed softly. "Which most of them aren't at the moment," he quipped.

"Dad, we're not running a nonprofit organization," Clay said softly. "The stockholders would scarcely understand our continuing to lease the shops at the old rates. They were low even before the hotel was re-modeled." He took a bite of toast and chewed slowly. "Besides," he continued when his mouth was empty, "their business can't help but increase as the hotel gets busier."

If they aren't in bankruptcy before this promised miracle takes place, Tracy thought grimly. She kept her eyes on her coffee cup, letting her internal rancor subside before she looked up again.

"And how long do you think this increased business at the hotel will take to trickle down to the shops in the hotel?" Her voice was surprisingly soft to her ears.

"Depends on the shopkeeper, to some degree, don't you think?" Clay replied.

"What does that mean?"

"I didn't wait for people to discover the hotel had been updated." Clay moved his cup aside for the waiter to lower a plate laden with a colorful omelette. "I suggest they also update their wares and do a little advertising. Look for new clientele." He smiled at Tracy as if the problem had been solved and turned his attention to the salsa-topped eggs.

Tracy closed her lips against a wry retort. Mr. Workaholic Winter probably expected Aunt Charli to paste her silver-and-scarlet logo advertising the chocolate shop on her hospital gown and pass out discount coupons to the doctors and nurses between pain pills. Irritated, she plunged her fork into a chunk of cantaloupe.

It was well after seven before Tracy found time to eat again. Few other diners occupied the hospital dining room. Past the dinner hour for employees, she surmised, sliding a cup of coffee and a plastic-wrapped sandwich on the Formica-topped table and sinking onto the coral-colored plastic cushion covering the seat of the metal chair. Ripples of weariness coursed across her back.

She hadn't stayed long at the candy shop. But she'd discovered a lot. Aunt Charli hadn't had insurance coverage for six months. She'd changed insurance companies, only to find she was no longer eligible for coverage. With her high blood pressure, overweight, and borderline diabetes, her application had been turned down.

To lower expenses, she'd let some of her employees go, keeping only Madge full time and two other employees part time. She'd thought she could manage until business picked up, Madge had said.

Tracy sipped the coffee, pondering the state of her aunt's finances. Aunt Charli's first groggy question after she'd returned from the recovery room was about business at the shop. "We usually see more customers on the weekend," she added hopefully.

"One lady even left because she had to wait a few

minutes in line,'' Tracy told her. She didn't add that
the middle-aged matron was irked at an elderly woman
dawdling before the candy display case like a child as
she selected an assortment of chocolates to take to her
grandchildren. The open door had also enticed a bored
fiftyish blond in white shorts and a Hawaiian-print
blouse tied across her ample midriff, who'd wandered
in to browse, and a couple of jeans-clad teenagers who
shook their heads when they noted the prices. Not exactly a mob, Tracy thought dourly. It was about the
amount of work Aunt Charli on crutches and her skel-
eton crew might handle. But the skeletal proceeds
would scarcely handle the rent! Leaving half the sandwich, Tracy carried her tray across the room to a con-
veyor belt leading to the kitchen.

Turning her pillow over for the tenth time in two
hours, Tracy turned her face away from the clock.
She'd decided to pay Charli's hospital bill, and she'd
think of other ways to help her aunt after she returned
to Taos. So why couldn't she sleep?

On Sunday, Aunt Charli's physician entered the
room in a sky blue jogging suit moments after Tracy
arrived.

"Glad you're here," he greeted her. "You can
shield me when I tell Charli I can't discharge her from
the hospital today."

"Aunt Charli is all right, isn't she?" Tracy peered
at the doctor anxiously.

"If you mean her general health, her hypertension
is under control with medication, but losing weight
would help. As for the ankle, I'd like her to stay in

the hospital a few days. She's having more pain than usual—which could be due to swelling." He looked at Charli solemnly. "I may need to cut the cast. Then we'll see about going home."

The band around Tracy's chest loosened. "Doesn't sound too serious, but I'll keep anything she can throw out of her reach." She grinned broadly at her aunt to assure her the words were frivolous. "She just told me she planned to go home on crutches today."

The physician looked at his patient in mock despair. "Sometimes I think a patient hears only what they want to hear. I said, more likely a wheelchair than crutches. You said you could handle that."

"I can." A faint trace of belligerence tinged Charli's voice.

"Is there someone to help at home?"

Tracy's eyes widened. "She lives alone," she blurted before Charli could answer.

"I can request a home-health nurse for a week or so. Insurance may cover a few visits." He grinned. "But they don't do windows. I doubt if they do dusting or cooking either. Perhaps a relative can stay with you," he suggested. "If not, talk to the nurse about contacting a registry for help." He paused as the beeper on his belt sounded. "You'll do fine," he said. Charli's lament that she had no insurance didn't reach his ears as he strode out the door and down the hall.

Before Tracy could assemble her thoughts, a white-frocked young woman bounced through the doorway. "Time for a bath?" she announced jovially.

Tracy grinned cheerfully at her aunt. "I'll try the coffee in the dining room while you get washed and polished."

Sitting in the sparsely occupied dining room, staring at the coffee cooling in a Styrofoam cup, Tracy felt far from cheerful. Aunt Charli wasn't overwhelmed with relatives. She had two nephews on her deceased husband's side, who called annually and sent cards at Christmas. She had Tracy, who had a plane ticket back to Taos on the late flight.

Tracy lifted the coffee and sipped carefully. It tasted as bad as her mood. She drank half the coffee and reached in her purse for her address book. She had little choice except to stay in Costa Corona a few more days—maybe until the end of the week. She could help in the shop, maybe even think of a way to increase the revenue. The thought of Aunt Charli's landlord intruded amidst her musings, despite her effort to ignore it. By the time she'd finished her coffee, asking for two weeks off seemed prudent. Maybe three, she amended as she searched for a telephone. Bryce had other part-timers who could fill in.

Strangely, her mood lightened. She 〳　ed briskly back to Charli's room, anxious to tell h　　her decision.

Aunt Charli sat, propped up by the tilt the hospital bed, applying a fresh layer of Lowering the tube, she looked at Tracy with twinkling eyes. "Clay told me you had breakfast with him yesterday."

"Clay came to visit you?"

"Dressed in a jogging suit." She grinned. "He must have been in the hotel flower shop before it opened." She gestured toward a colorful arrangement of flowers with two Mylar balloons attached. "Said he hoped you'd be in Costa Corona a while."

"I've been thinking about that. Staying a week could help you get organized to handle things from a wheelchair."

Relief flooded Charli's eyes. "I was a little worried about running the shop."

"Madge can do that. I'll stay with you."

"Where do you think I'll be?" Charli chortled.

"At the shop," Tracy said with an air of resignation. A minute later, she realized what that foreboded. If she was staying with Aunt Charli and Aunt Charli was staying at the shop, it might prove a little difficult to avoid Clay Winter. She'd have to work on that. She had no doubt that avoiding Clay was in her heart's best interest.

Chapter Three

Charli's Chocolates was a small, compact store that used space thriftily without appearing crowded to the customer. Ample room allowed the discriminating shopper to stand back and survey the display of rich, dark truffles, raspberry-laced bonbons, and variety of other sinfully rich sweets. Moving a few feet, the shopper could browse between two small, lace-covered tables topped with artfully packaged sweets. Many of the wares were displayed to induce hotel guests to buy for spouses at home, matrons to order for luncheon parties and wedding receptions, or grandmothers to lavish on their grandchildren. The prices weren't in keeping with the average teenage allowances.

Monday morning, Tracy stood behind the meticulously clean glass case studying the display when

Madge arrived. "Thought I'd look around a bit before you opened," she explained.

Madge turned the OPEN sign toward the sidewalk and closed the heavy glass door. "I called Charli. She is ecstatic, to put it mildly, that you are staying for a week." Madge glanced at Tracy warmly. "It's a nice thing to do."

Tracy lowered her gaze and peered intently at a green latticed basket filled with chocolate blueberries on the top shelf of the glass case. "This place isn't exactly wheelchair friendly." She lifted her lashes and waved her hand at the narrow space between the counter and the wall separating the kitchen from the shop. "Not that it will keep Aunt Charli away. But she'll need someone to drive her here and . . ." Tracy shrugged. "I thought I might be some help around the shop."

"Where do you want to start, kitchen or counter?" Madge reached inside the kitchen door and withdrew a handful of white cloth. She shook the bundle, revealing a lengthy cotton apron and a short, frilled serving apron.

Tracy reached for the less serviceable bit of cloth. "I can wait on customers, but you'd better teach me what to do in the kitchen before you turn me loose in there."

"Making chocolates hasn't changed since your aunt taught you. You'll do fine." Madge held forth the serving apron. "You'll find the prices listed at the back of the trays in the display case. I think all the other items are priced on the package or bin." She donned the longer apron, pulling the strings around to tie over her ample waist. "I'll start a batch of fudge."

After Madge left, Tracy looked out the glass windows at the people parading the sidewalk. Some paused to study the wares inside before moving on; others barely glanced at the enticing tidbits on display. Tracy wrinkled her forehead. Perhaps the delectable-looking wares appeared too expensive for a casual shopper, she mused. Or was it the shop's location in the corner of the elegant hotel?

She went back to the display case. Trays stacked with a variety of truffles in dainty pleated paper cups filled two shelves. Tracy noticed her favorite cocoa-dusted truffles in abundant supply, as well as a pyramid of white chocolates shaped like miniature snowballs. Another shelf supported mounds of pecan turtles and slabs of rich, dark fudge. Chocolate-covered blueberries filled a medium-sized bin. Tracy opened the glass door to lift a gilded net and peer at the half dozen seashell-shaped chocolates packaged inside. She breathed in the aroma of chocolate wafting around her, and the familiar fragrance brought back a wave of nostalgia. Her childhood hadn't been as lonely as she sometimes thought. To be honest, Aunt Charli had always seemed to be there, coating her with love as heavily as she coated her incomparable fudge balls with a rich, smooth mixture of chocolate.

Placing the package back on the tray, Tracy stared at it reflectively for a moment before she moved to the other side of the case. On the lace-clad tables, decorative baskets held containers shaped like bananas and oranges, filled with cream-colored and orange jelly beans. Another held mammoth chocolate suckers shaped like animals. Tracy lifted a chocolate horse and looked at the price. Lowering it back into the basket, she surmised it was one of the items packaged to attract doting grandmothers.

Clay's voice echoed in her mind. What had he said about advertising and attracting new customers? She sighed. Attracting a few more grandmothers would scarcely increase Aunt Charli's income enough to cover the rent. Clay might be a marketing marvel in the hotel industry, but she doubted enough customers could squeeze in front of the candy case to help in three months. For a moment, she pondered pleading for more time for Aunt Charli. But Charli, whose independent streak was as wide as her own, would find that as repugnant as Tracy did. Tracy was already worrying about how to pay the hospital bill without offending her beloved aunt. Her gaze roved over the chocolates. Charli wouldn't accept money to keep the shop open. If she was going to help Aunt Charli, it would have to be by helping the business. A week wasn't much time.

Rounding the case, she paused at the opening leading to the kitchen and leaned against the doorjamb. Madge bent over a large copper kettle, stirring the contents.

"Madge, I was wondering," she said nonchalantly. "Does the hotel place little chocolate mints or something on the pillows when the bed is turned down in the evening?"

"I've never stayed in the hotel."

"So if it does, it doesn't buy them from us," Tracy mused.

She didn't hear if Madge answered. Two middle-aged ladies entered the shop, and their voices echoed across the room. By the time she had boxed truffles for a bridal shower and related the reason for Charli's absence to the woman who said she was a frequent customer, two teenagers came in to browse.

At ten, an attractive young woman near Tracy's age hurried through the open door, nodded at Tracy, and sprinted around the counter to enter the kitchen. "Sorry," Tracy heard her say breathlessly. "The school bus was late." A few minutes later, she reappeared in the doorway, her face turned toward the kitchen. "Where do you want me to work today?"

Carrying a towel, Madge lumbered beside the newcomer and spoke to Tracy.

"Meet Sonjia." Madge dried her hands as she introduced the new arrival. "She comes to work after she gets her kindergartner off to school and leaves at noon in time to pick her up. Lindon comes at one, after his last class at the community college. He handles the counter after five and closes the shop at eight."

Tracy smiled at the young woman, murmuring a polite greeting before she spoke to Madge. "Is that all the employees Aunt Charli has now?"

"She let Bruce—he was full time—and the other part-timers go. Told them she'd call them back if business picked up." Madge spread her hands, palms up.

"Well, I guess we'll have to do something to see that business picks up."

"Do you want Sonjia to work the counter while you get acquainted with the kitchen?" Madge asked.

"Good idea." Tracy reached to untie her apron, but

Sonjia was already pulling a lacy half-circle from beneath the cash register counter.

Tracy walked through the doorway behind the counter to enter the small kitchen where Charli's candies were made. The kitchen was familiar to her; she'd followed Aunt Charli for years, watching her deftly hand-dip chocolates or carefully stir the couverture. The first time she had begged Charli to let her help, she had scorched the dark, glossy mixture. She learned much later how to blend warm cream with the mixture to make ganache. The old marble-topped counter for making fudge was still the same, but she noticed new tops had replaced the Formica she remembered. A second microwave oven had been added. But the old stove was the same. She touched the familiar surface. When she was a teenager, Charli had let her work on Saturdays, alternating between the stove and the candy display case. She pursed her lips. She should be able to remember something about the business, she told herself.

Aunt Charli was asleep, the head of the hospital bed raised and the speaker to the television rattling softly on her chest. Careful not to wake her, Tracy lowered her weary body in the armchair beside the bed. She'd worked in the kitchen most of the day, surprised to find it was almost seven o'clock when she paused. She was further surprised that she'd enjoyed it. Not that she meant to make it a habit, she assured herself on the way to the hospital. No workaholic's hours for her. She'd put in a little overtime for Charli—like taking a vacation from her relaxed lifestyle.

She lifted her gaze to the flickering television

screen, watching a silver-haired newscaster shuffle a few papers before he spoke. She didn't hear him. Her thoughts were on the chocolate shop that seemed in as much trouble as the hotel had been before Clay had taken over the management. Bring back old customers and court new ones, he'd said about the hotel. She watched the weatherman appear on the lighted screen without listening to his report. New customers? Squinting her eyes, she stared into space. Why couldn't Winter's Inn be one of them? Chocolate mints didn't say much. But she knew cocoa-dusted truffles would probably be too expensive for giveaway treats.

She ran her tongue over her lips and looked at the ceiling dreamily. If she was going to sell her idea to Clay Winter, she had to consider cost—the cost of making the product and the price he'd pay when it came to purchasing. Something small, but reflective of the hotel. She thought of the meeting rooms named after flowers and the lovely arrangements throughout the hotel. She shelved the idea of a floral design and thought of the sea and the seashore. Her thoughts progressed to the assortment of seashells in the collector's case in the lobby. And the chocolate shells in the gilded fishnet.

With growing excitement, Tracy stared at the sleeping figure of her aunt, willing her to awaken. In the hallway, the sound of a patient call bell, beeping with urgent regularity, was drowned momentarily by the ring of a telephone and laughter from a passing employee. Aunt Charli continued her regular, relaxed breathing.

Tracy returned to her musing. If the shell-shaped

chocolates were packaged individually and placed atop a pillowcase, wouldn't they make an attractive treat for an overnight guest? Tracy embellished on the idea. Why not put them in nature's seashells and wrap them in cellophane?

By the time her aunt awoke, she was eager to discuss the new idea. Groggily, Aunt Charli agreed with everything Tracy suggested.

Only after Tracy had started back to the shop did she question her aunt's groggy acquiescence. By that time, it was too late to check her enthusiasm. She'd make a sample product this evening—surely one of the shops that sold sacks of seashells to tourists was open.

Lindon had dimmed the lights and was on his way to the door when Tracy returned to the shop. Bidding him a hasty good night, she closed the door after him, turned the OPEN sign away from the sidewalk, and carried her packages to the kitchen.

It shouldn't take long to make the shells once she found the molds used for the chocolate cache in the golden net, she mused. Thoughts of the dark-eyed man whom she planned to receive the chocolates roved through her mind as she rummaged through the neatly arranged shelves. Leaving the shelf contents in mild disarray, she finally located the plastic molds.

She placed the molds on the counter in readiness and reached to turn on the small radio nearby. A melody floated softly across the room, and Tracy smiled at the familiarity of the old tune. Apparently the dial was set at Charli's favorite station. She wondered what kind of music Clay liked, and if he danced to slow or fast tunes. He'd be a good dancer, she reasoned. He'd circulated with easy grace across the crowded Hibiscus Room. For a moment, she wondered how it would feel to have his strong arms around her as they glided across a polished floor. She twirled and two-stepped across the small kitchen floor to collect a container of chocolate, a bowl, and a plastic spoon. Cradling the supplies and utensils in her arms, she waltzed back, swaying in front of the microwave oven as the tune ended. Shaking her head at her impulsive behavior, she plopped the container and bowl on the counter. The only way she wanted to see Clay Winter was across a desk in his office.

Shutting out the sound of the music, as well as thoughts of Clay, she concentrated on reading the directions for melting the chocolate and then setting the timer before she stirred the mixture. She was surprised to find she had the molds filled with two dozen dark, satiny shells ready to slide into the refrigerator in less than twenty minutes.

Pleased with her work, she opened the package of seashells and put the contents in the sink to wash. Next, she looked for cellophane and stickers. Waiting for the chocolate shells to set, she polished an abalone shell until the pink-and-green mother-of-pearl lining sparkled. She planned to use it as a container for the netted shells.

Humming softly to the music, she gave a final polish to the lining. She wondered if wrapping the chocolates in different colors of cellophane, perhaps the pale pink and mint green of the abalone shell, would enhance the package. She tightened her lips, scrutinizing the shell. Maybe the whole thing wasn't such a good idea. She could imagine keepsake boxes of assorted name-brand chocolates would be Clay's preference when he sent gifts, despite his insistence that Charli made the best chocolates in California. How did she think she could entice him to buy her homemade idea?

Doubt clouding her spirits, she unmolded the assortment of chocolates on a tea towel. Looking at the shapes that resembled whelks, olive shells, western Atlantic concs, scallops, clams, cockles, and some shells she couldn't name, she couldn't help but feel a glow of pleasure brighten the cloud. By the time she'd placed a chocolate shell inside each washed and dried scallop shell, her elation had returned, allowing her to peer at the candy with a thought to the finished product. She covered the packages in cellophane and sealed them with Charli's scarlet-and-silver seals. Pleased with the appearance, she wrapped the remaining chocolates, placed them in the abalone shell, and covered the contents with clear plastic. She took a moment to scrutinize her handiwork before she placed it in a silver gift box and firmly added one of Charli's business cards.

She refused to let self-doubt rise again to mar her excitement. Hershey's Kisses may have started with one small idea. Suddenly, the thought of Clay Winter's attractively molded lips bobbed up with the thought of kisses.

Placing the box on a corner of the countertop, she thought about her plan. Tomorrow she'd send the package to Clay's office, with a note to his secretary requesting an appointment. She straightened the scarlet-and-silver ribbon on the box. She hoped Clay was as fond of Charli's chocolates as he claimed. She could use all the help she could get.

It was almost noon on Tuesday before Clay's secretary called Tracy to say Clay had gone to Los Angeles on business, but he'd be happy to have dinner with her at six-thirty at the hotel.

Tracy hesitated. She wanted to see him in his office. She'd worked half the night on a speech to sell him her seashell chocolates, and she wanted it to be all business. Just seeing him tied her tongue in satin-slippery ribbons. She didn't want her resolve further weakened by wine, food, and music. The secretary's voice interrupted her chaotic thoughts.

"Mr. Winter said to tell you he is sorry it is an early dinner, but he has an eight o'clock meeting."

Tracy swallowed. "Six-thirty will be fine."

"Do you like seafood?"

Tracy replied she did and replaced the receiver. Six-thirty to eight in the hotel dining room, and Clay had to rush off to another meeting. She could handle that. It might even be better than trying to rush through her rehearsed speech in five minutes in his office.

Tracy went to see Aunt Charli at two, delighted to find her room filled with visitors. She couldn't discuss her plans with Aunt Charli now, she told herself. Besides, she might not be successful. No need to build up Aunt Charli's hopes. It was a minor thing anyway. Not enough to affect the cash flow too much. Finding a break in the conversation, she dangled the car keys, telling Aunt Charli she had to return with the station wagon so Lindon could pick up supplies, and left the room.

*   *   *

At six, Tracy exchanged the painted T-shirt and jeans she'd worn to work for a skirt and blouse. Viewing her attire in the mirror over the spotless porcelain sink, she sighed. The turquoise blouse blended well with the flowing multicolored midcalf-length skirt, but it was scarcely a business suit. Brushing her hair briskly and giving her pale lips a new coat of color, she called to let Lindon know she was leaving.

Clay Winter, charcoal clouds floating on a tie to match his tailored silk suit, greeted Tracy warmly as she stepped off the elevator. The look of admiration in his eyes brought forth the satin ties to bind her tongue.

"Thank you for the chocolates."

Tracy accepted his gratitude with a nod, trying to get a grip on herself.

He grinned humorously. "Is this something new in the women's movement? I thought men traditionally sent flowers and chocolates." He touched her arm briefly to guide her toward the seafood restaurant.

How could she come up with a responsive quip with her heartbeat interfering with her head? Tracy thought wildly. She wanted her reply to be light and uninformative. Until she was ready to spring the seashell idea. She wanted his full attention when she approached the subject of supplying chocolate treats to the hotel's guests. On the verge of stuttering, she took a sigh of relief at the appearance of the maître d'.

Following the black-trousered man, she glanced at her surroundings. Fisherman's Cove was a casual room furnished in someone's idea of a seaside sip and dine. Aged barrels, polished to a satin sheen, served as cocktail tables. High, broad-backed peacock chairs, their cushions emblazoned with green leaves and orange bird-of-paradise blossoms, cozily encased the cocktail customers. Secluded mahogany booths filled two walls, and a few tables, shielded by five-foot ficus plants, occupied places near the windows. Beyond the glass doors, on a small balcony, blue-cushioned chairs and tables resplendent in white and navy linens gave their occupants a view of the Pacific Ocean. Japanese lanterns wavered overhead in the breeze and hurricane lamps atop each table waited to be lit for the evening.

Clay spoke to the maître d' and swept one hand toward a secluded table with a view of the ocean.

Tracy sat down tensely. Feeling Clay's gaze, she admired the delicate arrangement of carnations and baby's breath, her slow perusal pausing on the decorative lamp. *Scarcely the setting for a business meeting,* she worried. Her first impulse had been right. She would have been better able to pursue her goal had she been sitting across a desk from him dressed in a straight skirt and matching jacket. But it had been two years since she'd owned a business suit. She unfolded the navy napkin and smoothed it over her bohemian skirt, knowing she could not avoid looking at Clay much longer.

Looking up, she had a reprieve when the maître d' handed them oversize green-and-gold menus. Moments later a youthful waiter appeared, pencil poised over his tablet as he told them about the specials of the day, his words as carefully spaced as if he were reciting a poem memorized for classroom oration. Clay nodded and thanked him without the faintest quiver of his lips. But Tracy caught the glint of humor in his eyes before he turned his gaze to the oversize menu.

"The bouillabaisse is quite good," Clay said. "The grilled shrimp and scallops are very tasty, and you have to try the house dressing on the green salad to believe it."

After giving their orders to the waiter, Clay waited for the wine steward to pour wine into their glasses, tasted it, and settled his gaze on Tracy.

"I thought you would be on your way back to Taos." He leaned forward, his eyes flecked with grains of gold from the light reflected off the centerpiece.

"I couldn't leave Aunt Charli in the hospital."

"Understandable. When is she coming home?"

"I'm not sure. The doctor said she must stay a few more days."

"I hope nothing is wrong, but I'm glad you're staying around for a few more days."

"A little longer, I'm afraid. I can't leave Aunt Charli to cope with a broken ankle and"—Tracy took a fortifying breath—"possible eviction."

"Eviction?"

"I believe you told your father you weren't running a charity operation, or something like that. I took that to mean Aunt Charli must pay these exorbitant new rent or get out."

Clay lifted his glass, his eyes darkening as he examined the wine. "I don't believe those were my exact words."

"Near enough." Tracy clenched her fists at the clipped reply. This was not the way to approach a prospective customer.

He looked at her for a long moment, the somber look in his eyes softening. "Perhaps we can work something out with Charli."

"You know Aunt Charli." Tracy made her voice light. "She wouldn't accept charity. She'd want to pay just like the other tenants."

Clay's eyes narrowed. "Does the chocolate package you sent to my office have something to do with this conversation?"

Tracy moved her hands to her knees, pressing her nails into the thin fabric of her skirt. "Business," she said succinctly.

Leaning back, Clay rested his tanned forearms on the broad woven arms of his chair. "Perhaps you'd better elaborate."

Tracy took a deep, determined breath and looked at him steadily. "Do you offer evening treats to your guests when the beds are turned down?"

"I believe so." Clay waited patiently.

"Something special?"

"Mints, I believe. Chocolate-dipped strawberries in the suites."

"Chocolate seashells are slightly more distinctive."

"Chocolate seashells like the ones I've seen in Charli's shop?"

Tracy nodded. "I figure Charli's Chocolates could supply you at a reasonable cost."

He tipped his head. "How much do you know about making candy and calculating costs?"

"I think I mentioned I practically grew up in Aunt Charli's candy kitchen."

"Sampling the wares, or did you do something more practical?"

"I can melt chocolate without scorching it."

"It's more than I can do," Clay said humorously. Laughter sparkled in his eyes and Tracy couldn't help sharing his humor.

Tracy leaned back as a waiter returned, grateful for his presence. It gave her time to regain her composure. By the time he had served Clay and withdrawn, she had found her place in the mentally prepared speech. "You said the shopkeepers should look for new business."

Clay raised an eyebrow. "Is this Charli's idea?"

"Not exactly."

"Yours?"

She nodded.

"Selling me seashell treats for my hotel guests is your way of getting new business?"

"It's a start." Tracy echoed Clay's earlier words.

Clay picked up his salad fork, peering at her silently for a moment. When he spoke, his voice held no emotion. "Send me the figures. I'll get back to you by the end of the week." He raised the fork. "With business out of the way, I want you to taste that dressing. I've been trying to get the recipe from the chef for a week."

"I thought you couldn't keep chocolate from burning." Tracy grinned.

"Salads don't have to be cooked. And I know my way around a barbecue grill."

"Which is more than I can say." Tracy laughed softly.

"Sounds like we'd make a good team. I can cook entrées and you can make desserts."

Tracy felt her heartbeat quicken. Getting emotionally involved with Clay wasn't what she had in mind. She stabbed at a red-tipped leaf of radicchio, lifting it to her mouth and lowering her lashes as if savoring the taste.

"The dressing is good." She caught her tongue before she could ask him to share the recipe if he managed to get it. She didn't want to get friendly with him. When your head told you a man wasn't right for you, the smart thing to do was keep your heart as far away as possible. This evening was nice, but tomorrow she'd leave the financial figures with his secretary. She'd have no need to see him again. Charli would sign a contract or whatever shopkeepers did under the circumstances.

Casually, she turned the conversation to the variety of seashells in the collector's case in the hotel lobby. She was surprised to discover Clay had started the collection when he was fourteen. She was further surprised when their conversation was interrupted by the youthful waiter wheeling a delectable cart of desserts to their table. Tracy glanced at her watch quickly. Where had the time gone? She'd worried about filling an hour with conversation, and now it was almost time for Clay's meeting. She looked at Clay to see him smiling at her.

"The chocolate mousse looks marvelous."

Tracy returned his grin. "And you'll be late for your meeting," she warned. She looked at the waiter and shook her head at the myriad of offerings.

Waiting for Clay to sign for the meal, she looked out at the ocean view, telling herself to stop feeling so ridiculously happy. Clay hadn't made any commitments about the seashell chocolates. So why was her heart pumping overtime to make her head dizzy?

Tracy stood, not sure whether or not to shake his hand as if they were business acquaintances. She decided against it. Touching him was not a good idea. ''Thank you for the dinner.'' Her voice was professionally polite. ''The salad and scallops were as good as you said.''

''My pleasure.'' His eyes seconded his words.

Tracy looked away. Even his look was unnerving. Clutching her purse, she bade him good night, added a few words about having the figures on his desk soon, and looked across the room. ''My car is in the parking lot at the back of the hotel,'' she said a little breathlessly. ''I can go out through the patio.''

''Good idea,'' Clay said. He followed her across the room. ''I need a little salt air before I go into another air-conditioned room.'' He looked down when they reached the gateway, grinning at the delicate straps holding heels and thin soles of leather to her feet. ''It might be easier for you to have the valet bring your car to the front.''

She grinned. ''They're sturdier than they look.''

Clay motioned toward a wrought-iron gate on one side of the patio. ''We can leave this way,'' he said.

Passing by two couples dining on the patio, Clay led the way to the gate. A breeze from the ocean ruffled the serrated leaves of boxed Kentia palms on the patio and spread fragrance from a gardenia plant in a half-barrel container. After descending the steps with Clay beside her, Tracy paused on the concrete path that curved around the building to the parking lot and the beach and back to the side of the hotel, waiting for Clay to close the gate.

She felt a rush of warmth as his hand cupped her elbow, guiding her along the neon-lit walk. The breeze was stronger now, uninhibited by rails and potted plants, and the air smelled of salt and sea. Across the sand, a trickle of laughter erupted from a bikini-clad girl tossing a Frisbee to a sun-bronzed young man with youthful fervor.

Leaving the shelter of the building, Tracy followed the path toward the parking lot, slowing at the sight of a string of caution lights reinforcing their message with a barrier of sawhorses.

Clay's grip on her arm tightened. "I'm sorry. I forgot maintenance people are working on this end of the lot. We'll have to detour through the sand." He released her arm to wave at her heels. "I could play the part of Sir Walter Raleigh, but I don't think my coat is long enough."

"I don't need to be coddled. I'm a twentieth-century gal." Tracy laughed, balancing one hip lightly against a sawhorse to bend and grasp the strap on her sandal. As she released the buckle, the sawhorse shifted.

The startled sound she emitted was stifled as Clay's arms caught her, holding her briefly to allow her to regain her balance. Before she could say thank you, she felt the warmth of his hands closing around her ankle to lift her foot and remove the sandal. Warmth rising through her, she kept her hand firmly on the sawhorse, resisting the urge to touch his sturdy shoulder.

Dangling her slippers on one finger, he stood up. A shaft of moonlight struck his face, highlighting his sensuous lips, and Tracy drew in a breath. For a second, the reason that she was here with him was forgotten, and only the look of his lips filled her mind as she wondered how they would feel against hers.

She reached for the shoes, laughing when he pulled them back teasingly. Grabbing at his hand ineptly, her fingers entwined with his amid the straps, lashing them together. She could feel her pulse racing. He looked at her then, and despite the effort, she couldn't look away. Mesmerized, she felt Clay gently thread her slender fingers out of the leather web. She still looked at him as he lifted one hand and smoothed the breeze-swept hair back from her forehead. Her thoughts went on hold like a tape recorder with the pause button activated. Unwillingly, her gaze lowered to his lips. A burst of laughter followed by the swish of a Frisbee sailing overhead brought her down to earth with a jolt. She stepped back, clearing her throat as if to clear her body of the momentary lapse. Holding up the sandals, she smiled brightly. "Thank you. You don't have to walk me to the car and fill your shoes with sand. I'll be fine." She rummaged in her purse, trying to locate the station wagon keys while she waited for the youthful young man to jog past her to retrieve the saucer-shaped Frisbee.

Emitting a sigh, she looked at Clay in embarrassment. "I'm afraid I have to walk back with you." She grimaced. "I just remembered . . . Lindon hung the keys to Aunt Charli's car on the key rack when he returned from picking up supplies. I forgot to get them." She held up her wrist, turning it to catch a ray of light. "I hope I can catch him before he locks up."

She found Lindon turning out the lights when she

approached the shop. Waving to Clay, she entered the shop to retrieve the keys. She was surprised to find Clay in the shop when she returned from the kitchen.

"I'll wait for you to lock up."

Tracy nodded, detouring to open the display case and lift out a pleated cup containing a dark ball of rich chocolate.

"The least I can do is offer you the dessert you missed."

"Thank you, kind lady. You must know I'm partial to Charli's truffles." He lifted the candy and took a small bite. Closing his eyes briefly, he made a small, pleasurable sound. Then he lifted the chocolate toward Tracy's mouth. "I wouldn't think of not sharing." His fingers touched her lips as he pressed the morsel forward.

Meeting his magnetic gaze, Tracy nibbled on the truffle. She moved to pull away and the chocolate smeared across her mouth. She laughed, shaking her head in protest. "I've sampled enough candy today."

He reached forward and brushed one finger softly across her lips. Looking at her, he raised the chocolate-smeared finger to his mouth and tasted it.

Tracy caught her breath, unable to look away for a moment. Then she blinked and moved toward the door. "Wouldn't want you to be late for your meeting." She held the door open for him, locked it after him, waved, and left him standing on the sidewalk as she walked briskly and blindly to the parking lot.

He's not the man for you, she told herself. He's handsome, charming, thoughtful, and industrious. The industrious part was the rub. She focused on the sidewalk. Common sense told her avoiding him was the only way to keep her heart intact when her body wouldn't cooperate. But to help Charli, she needed to court him as a client!

Her thoughts were spinning as she turned into Aunt Charli's garage with the feeling of Clay's fingers lingering on her lips.

Chapter Four

Clay stood before his desk and lifted the cup of coffee he'd brought from the restaurant to his lips, tasting the fresh, hot liquid. He placed the cup on the desk with approval. Pulling his daily calendar to the center of his desk, he ran a forefinger swiftly over the noted appointments and grimaced. He should be in a Wednesday breakfast meeting with a number of Chamber of Commerce members. How could he have forgotten?

He glanced at his watch. A little late to leave now; the meeting would be in progress. He walked around the desk, lowered his body into the high-backed leather chair, and reached out to reclaim the coffee cup. Taking a long, slow swallow, he looked out the window at the palm frond–draped view. Even if he left now, by the time he found a parking space the meeting would be half over. Perhaps he wouldn't be missed. He pulled the calendar near and scribbled a notation to contact a fellow member later and get a report on plans for the summer festival. He looked at the coffee cup and made another note to mention the excellent brew to the café manager.

He'd stopped by the coffee shop, a habit he'd formed by finding time to walk through the various restaurants and departments occasionally as a way to let the personnel know he was interested in every facet of the hotel. Not that his assistants didn't perform to his satisfaction. But it didn't hurt to personally note the appearance of the shop or the service rendered. He knew he was a workaholic. Thinking of business first was automatic. So how had he completely back-shelved the breakfast appointment?

He drained the cup and stared into space. It hadn't been difficult. His night had been filled with fantasies of Tracy McMillan, not business.

As if waiting on the sidelines of his mind, her wide smile and the carefree sound of her laughter echoed in his thoughts. Yet, he mused, despite her avowed pursuit of fun and laughter, she hadn't hesitated to throw herself into helping Charli. She was an enigma, which made her even more entrancing.

Shaking his head, he opened a drawer, withdrew a folder, and placed it on the desk. *Enough daydreaming, Winter.* Yet, he stared at it without lifting the cover. Knowing Tracy worked under the same roof as he did might make concentration a little elusive for the next few days. The thought of passing within a few feet of her each day brought a sense of excitement. He'd wanted to kiss her last night—he had kissed her in his dreams—but he could see she was wary. The buzzword in courting her might well be caution.

Then again, she insisted she was returning to Taos. Not only was long-distance courting difficult, in his case it was near impossible. Even when he was sleeping, his pager and telephone were on alert to keep him in touch with the hotel. He swiveled his chair to look out the window at the distant ocean. His view caught only a wedge of water laced with the drooping, serrated strands of a coconut palm landscaping the grounds beneath his window. Picture-postcard views of sun-jeweled seawater came under the heading of revenue. As did his time. So he'd have to make the time Tracy planned to be in Costa Corona count. Or find a way to keep the cautious lady from Taos around.

Dressed in a fresh T-shirt and jeans, Tracy passed by the shop without stopping to call out to Madge. She wanted to get to Clay's office and leave the figures for the chocolate treats with his secretary before he arrived.

The outer door to the reception area was open and she hurried inside, relieved to find the secretary away from her desk. She wouldn't have to explain the envelope's contents. Leaning forward, she placed the envelope on the uncluttered surface and heard a deep, familiar voice call her name. Startled, her hand jerked, then, despite her previous anxiety to avoid Clay, a wave of pleasure swept over her. Withdrawing the envelope, she turned.

"Good morning." She held the envelope up, hoping the shaky feeling in her chest didn't extend to her fingers. "You suggested I submit some numbers regarding the seashell chocolate project."

Clay stood up. A broad smile split his tanned face, flashing pinpoints of pleasure in his eyes.

"Bring them in." He extended his hand for the envelope, his look catching her in a splash of sunlight from the window. Unaware of his suspended breath, his gaze roved over her face. Beneath the pert nose, the tip of her tongue touched her full lips and withdrew so quickly he thought he might have imagined it. With the barest hint of bravado, she tilted her chin, setting earrings of tiny turquoise balls and tinsel-thin silver rods dancing amid the sun-dappled golden hair. For a second he felt mesmerized, clutching the envelope as if trying to capture the warmth of the hand that had held it a moment before. Then he looked away and motioned her to sit in a dark blue upholstered chair opposite him.

"You didn't have to stay up late to get this to me," he said in a surprisingly businesslike tone. "You're not in competition with anyone on this." He opened the envelope and sat down.

"It didn't take long." Tracy lowered her hands to her lap, nervously threading her fingers together, and forced herself not to dampen her dry lips again with a nervous tongue. No need to mention she'd worked on the proposal before she'd gone to dinner with him, or that it had taken longer than she'd expected. She found the business knowledge she'd used two years ago slightly rusty. Only the reminder that the effort was for Aunt Charli kept her redoing the figures.

She watched his gaze as he perused the papers. She'd set the price per unit to make a good profit for

Aunt Charli. Then she'd lowered it for fear Clay would find it too high to consider. Setting it aside, she'd retrieved it five minutes later to check everything again, fearing she'd used retail instead of wholesale prices from the supply list at the shop to calculate the cost. Still nervous, she'd rechecked the ingredient amounts.

She'd glanced at the completed columns last night and again this morning with trepidation. But she hadn't changed one figure. The early morning memory of Clay's touch wasn't conducive to computerlike thinking. Nor was her alertness improving with her gaze focused on his lips. She lowered her eyes to concentrate on his hands. She looked up when he lowered the papers.

Setting them in front of him, Clay leaned back and rested his arms on the dark upholstery. "I'll have my assistant go over this. Costlier than mints but, as you pointed out, more distinctive."

Tracy loosened the grip on her fingers. "Thank you for taking the time to look at it." She pushed her feet against the floor, preparing to rise.

"Ah." Clay made a small sound and pinpointed his gaze on Tracy. "I've been thinking about your concern over Charli. I want to help, too. Charli is special to me." He tapped the fingers of his right hand against the soft leather. "Lowering Charli's rent might be a problem. The other shopkeepers could cry discrimination."

Tracy sat tensely on the edge of the chair, looking at him inquiringly.

"Increased revenue is the only answer."

"And you think selling a few seashells is like putting a Band-Aid against a crack in a seawall,'' Tracy said with a wry grin.

Clay lifted a forefinger to his chin, his eyes narrowing. ''You might try a few other things to back up the Band-Aid.''

Tracy felt her heart race. Any of which meant staying in the shop—under the same roof as the attractive CEO? Her throat tightened. ''For example?''

''Over-the-counter sales may not be enough. Charli needs to expand her sales to the business community.'' Clay's look met Tracy's, and for a moment he lost his train of thought. Grasping for straws, he thought of the missed Chamber of Commerce meeting. ''She knows lots of people. She's a member of the Chamber of Commerce.'' He paused, nodding as if he'd just had a brainstorm. Which he had. ''Approaching some of Charli's fellow members about providing chocolate surprises for their employees at Christmas, or maybe birthdays, is one idea.'' He beamed at Tracy.

Tracy looked reflective. ''It might work. Aunt Charli could make calls. She must have a list of telephone numbers if she is a member.'' She relaxed visibly, her lips responding to Clay's broad smile. ''If she gets any orders, she can rehire her old help. Thank you for the suggestion.''

Clay rubbed his forefinger up and down his chin. ''The idea might sell better if the members were approached personally. Telephone solicitations strike an unresponsive chord in a number of people.''

Tracy's smile flattened. ''That's a little out of the question, since Aunt Charli is in the hospital.''

''You aren't.''

''Me? I won't be here long. Besides, my experience

in selling amounts to ringing up sales for Taos tourists who are eager to buy a souvenir when they walk into the shop.''

''You sold me, and I wasn't eager to buy.''

Doubt clouded Tracy's eyes, darkening their violet-blue color.

Clay pursed his lips briefly. This was not the time to falter. He picked up a pen from his desk and rolled it slowly between his fingers. ''Our director of marketing is pursuing more meeting and conference business. You might think of the same approach in regard to supplying chocolate specialties to engagement parties, wedding receptions, and bar mitzvahs held in the hotel. Or maybe something artistic for the conference dinners. Some of them end their sessions with a gala affair, including awards or presentations, so the table decor is often complete with edible take-home treats for the guests. Not only weekend conferences; we have dinners for special occasions with small take-home tokens of the affair.'' He narrowed his eyes in reflection. ''A movie company recently celebrated the start of a new romance series with a dinner in the Camellia Room. I remember seeing chocolate hearts and chocolate flowers at each place setting. Quite attractive.''

Tracy shook her head with an air of uncertainty, setting the silver-and-turquoise earrings in motion.

Clay could almost see her en route to Taos. He rocked back in the swivel chair and glanced out the window casually before he focused his look on Tracy. ''I'm attending a luncheon in Newport Beach tomorrow. A friend who caters parties for a number of Hollywood celebrities will be there. I'd like you to meet him.''

He shifted the papers aside casually. ''Many of his clients are as fond of chocolate as I am, and being his supplier could be a boon to Charli. You don't have to do a hard sell. Just mention Charli is branching out and ask if you can send him some samples. No more trouble than you went through with the samples you sent me.''

''Chocolate seashells?'' Tracy looked unconvinced.

''No. I was thinking more in the line of Charli's truffles. And maybe something special like the white chocolate baskets I saw you make for a bridal shower at the hotel.''

''With Aunt Charli in a wheelchair, who's going to make these specialties?''

''I imagine Madge is quite proficient. Also, didn't you say Charli could call back her former workers?'' He widened his eyes, adding a disarming grin.

''I guess I could discuss it with Aunt Charli,'' Tracy said resignedly. She stood, anxious to leave before Clay could pursue his idea. ''Can I call you?''

''I'll be waiting breathlessly.'' Mischief sparkled in his eyes as the grin spread.

Tracy still felt the impact of his smile as she met the arriving secretary. Pausing to let her pass, she heard Clay's voice.

''Maria, is that you?''

The secretary nodded at Tracy and answered her boss.

''I'll need another reservation for the luncheon in Newport Beach tomorrow.''

The secretary grimaced. ''It's kinda' late.''

"Try," Clay called. "I have a lot of faith in your charm."

Leaving, Tracy headed for the bank of elevators. With luck on her side, maybe Clay wouldn't get another reservation. She shook her head in annoyance at herself. Why had she even considered accompanying him to a luncheon when she knew the effect he had on her? All she wanted was to help Charli out of her current jam and scramble back to New Mexico. She lifted her head to gaze at the lighted floor numbers above the elevator doors and nodded to herself. That's why she was considering spending a few hours with him. To help Aunt Charli. The sooner business improved, the sooner she could schedule a flight to Taos. Which was what she wanted, wasn't it?

She went to the hospital at lunchtime to see if the doctor had discharged Aunt Charli.

She was surprised when her aunt didn't moan "When am I gettin' outa' here" in greeting. Instead, she leaned back against the upraised head of the narrow hospital bed, animatedly discussing income taxes with a new roommate. She paused briefly to nod at Tracy, running a hand through her disordered hair. The usual bouffant rise was absent, and her strawberry-colored hair sagged despondently around her plump cheeks. But she'd deftly applied a shadow of rouge across her cheekbones and a brave splash of color to her lips. Finishing her sentence, she introduced Tracy to the other occupant in the room and then pushed at her hair again.

"Tracy, since you won't spirit me away from this place, at least find me a beautician who makes hospital calls. I'm embarrassed for the nurses to see me, let alone visitors.''

Tracy made no effort to suppress a teasing smile. ''Are you sure it's the visitors you're worried about?'' She chuckled. ''I've seen the physician who was on call last evening.'' She rolled her eyes with an extravagant sigh. ''That magnificent mane of silver on his head doesn't make him look older, just better. He's available, from what I overheard in the dining room. But you'll have to stand in line. A few of the hospital's female employees already have plans to change his bachelor status.''

Charli's mouth pursed and eyes the color of the pale blue bed jacket she wore sparkled in mock animosity. She retied the ribbons on her jacket with a flourish.

''I don't want to change his life-style, but I wouldn't mind if he stopped by the chocolate shop regularly. You said we needed more customers.'' Her eyes sparkled mischievously this time. ''I want to do my bit for your campaign.''

''I can't fault you there.'' Tracy lowered her body onto the straight-backed chair by the bed.

''Speaking of your campaign, anything new?''

Tracy hesitated. Should she tell Aunt Charli she'd submitted the bid to supply chocolates to the hotel, or should she wait? What if Clay turned the plan down? She'd have raised Charli's hopes needlessly.

''Clay Winter invited me to a luncheon in Newport Beach. He thinks I could meet a caterer friend of his who might purchase his sweet supplies from you.''

''That sounds like Clay. He's such a nice young man.'' She looked at Tracy as if for agreement. The lack of response didn't dampen her enthusiasm. ''I

think you should go. New contacts are important."
She paused, pushing the drooping hair upward. "You
know, we did supply chocolates for many of the affairs
at the hotel before people stopped scheduling parties
there. I'd like to do it again. Talking to this caterer
might just get us started again."

Tracy moaned, only partially in mock despair.
"Aunt Charli, I don't have anything to wear to a
luncheon. T-shirts and jeans or baggy blouses and
broomstick skirts are scarcely appropriate, and I have
no time to shop today." Nor any inclination, she
added silently.

Charli laughed. "Aha. I have a knowledgeable contact in the clothing business who is coming to visit
this afternoon."

Tracy smiled in resignation.

She hadn't been back in the shop an hour before
she received a call from the hospital. Or, rather, Rose.
Charli had been discharged.

"I've invited her to stay the rest of the week with
me. I'd welcome the company. Martin left on a trip
today and he'll be gone until the weekend. You have
enough to keep you busy helping in the shop right
now, and I could use a few days away from my shop."

After talking to her aunt and hanging up the telephone, Tracy realized she felt a sense of relief. She'd
worried about trying to convince Charli to stay away
from the shop a few days, but she'd worried more
about leaving her at home.

It was almost eleven o'clock Thursday morning before Tracy thought again of what she would wear to

the luncheon. She knew a plastic-covered garment sent from Rose Gaynor's shop hung in the mini–coat closet in the back, but the hours had been so busy that only Madge's repeated warnings finally sent her to change from jeans into whatever Rose had sent as suitable for a business luncheon. She'd almost hoped Clay wouldn't get a reservation for her, but he'd called less than an hour after she left his office.

Now he was standing outside the door to the chocolate shop, caught in conversation with someone who'd just hailed him.

A deluge of midday sun wove silver threads across the fabric of Clay's well-cut silk suit. Pursing her lips, Tracy assessed his attire against the cobalt blue linen from Chantilly Rose. She had no doubt it was appropriate. Not all of Rose's customers were those who summered at the beach, wintered in Palm Springs, and lived in Beverly Hills. Not many years ago, Rose had pointed out secretaries, screenwriters, and corporate vice presidents while Tracy hesitated over selecting a plain silk blouse.

Unconsciously Tracy smoothed the straight skirt over her hips, knowing the fitted jacket clung to her as if it had been cut to her measurements. So why was she dawdling in the shop, dreading for Clay to open the glass door and enter?

Clay stepped inside the store. He greeted her cheerfully, said hello to Madge, and then asked Tracy if she was ready to go. She nodded and preceded him out the door. On the way to the car, Clay paused as a groundskeeper neared. "How's the new baby, Don?"

For a moment, Tracy was surprised at his thoughtfulness. Then he asked about the condition of some newly planted palm trees and her admiration waned. The concern about his employee's child was a prelude to checking on business. As usual.

Clay steered his car away from the hotel drive and onto the coast highway, threading his way deftly through the heavy traffic. His beeper sounded five minutes later.

Automatically he reached toward the console and then grinned sheepishly. "My car phone's on the fritz. I'll have to remember to check in when we reach Newport Beach."

Nor did he forget. As soon as they arrived, he introduced her to a group of people, and asked to be excused, pointing to the beeper.

Returning shortly, he guided her slowly between groups of people talking and others looking for empty chairs. Then he saw the quarry he sought. Touching Tracy's arm, he motioned to a table in the distance and, moments later, introduced her to his caterer friend.

Despite the appealing look of the colorful and appetizing luncheon salads, Tracy found swallowing difficult. The caterer's interest in Charli's chocolates seemed to be related to his interest in Charli's niece. He indicated he had patronized the shop a few times for events at the hotel and he'd be delighted to discuss a new venture over dinner. He swept her polite hesitation aside and embarked on a new tactic.

"Could you show me some samples on Monday?" he queried.

When Tracy nodded, he added, "Plan to stay for lunch. You must sample my wares."

"Thank you," Tracy croaked. She glanced at Clay, as if for approval, and was surprised to see the scowl on his face. She thought he'd be pleased. She was getting new business, wasn't she?

Waiters removed plates and silverware quietly, and the microphone made strange noises as someone adjusted it. Clay leaned close to Tracy. She felt the warmth of his breath and caught hers. "Now you must pay for your lunch by listening to a few speakers," he teased.

"Maybe he'll know some good jokes," she whispered back.

"On disaster preparedness?"

"Disasters, like earthquakes?"

"Earthquakes, brush fires, and mud slides, to mention a few." He grinned and gazed into her eyes, blocking out the rest of the room. Then the speaker approached the podium and Clay leaned back, and Tracy remembered to breathe.

She controlled her lungs, exhaling slowly. But she could do little about the jogging pulse in her throat. She needed a disaster plan of her own, she mused, if she planned to stay around Clay Winter.

When the speaker concluded, Tracy lifted her handbag and prepared to rise. She spoke briefly to the caterer, nodded to the others at the table, and looked at her watch as if to suggest to Clay a need to leave. She doubted he would mind returning to the hotel, even if he did consider the meeting part of his job. Which it was, she admitted. As a hotelier, the need to be aware of new ways to protect his guests was a priority. She didn't expect his smug smile as she turned away from the caterer. He stood, cupped her elbow in a propietary grasp, and escorted her to the door.

"Howard seems interested," he teased, taking her arm again as they stepped into the warm air.

"I hope so. Aunt Charli will be pleased." She risked a glance at him. Why did she get the feeling he wasn't talking about chocolates?

"You didn't eat much."

"I did," she said defensively. Now was he suggesting the caterer's attentions had curbed her appetite? She pulled her arm free and walked briskly to the car. He did not touch her again when he opened the car door, but the feel of his eyes on her face sent ripples through her. He walked around the car and slid behind the steering wheel.

Switching on the motor, he waited until he'd pulled into traffic to speak again. "I used to find it hard to eat at business meetings, too. Now I try to get in a bite between conversations." He swung the car easily around a slow-moving carload of boisterous young people, avoided an approaching van, and slid easily back into the traffic lane.

Tracy relaxed slightly. "Since I don't plan to make a career of business luncheons, I doubt if I'll lose any weight."

"I hope not." Humor tinged his tone. "It would be difficult to improve . . ." He hesitated. "On your present weight," he finished lamely.

Tracy restrained a giggle. The competent, in-charge CEO was embarrassed.

"You look fine the way you are," he said in a stronger voice. "Changing the subject, did I mention we're expecting our first conference group since the reopening of the hotel the weekend after this? Better stock up on your souvenir chocolates.''

Tracy sighed. Did he never stop talking about work? ''Are you trying to coerce me into becoming a work freak too?''

''Is there an easier way to success?''

''I don't want to be a success.''

''Everyone wants to be a success.'' He raised his voice slightly to overpower the tuneless drumming erupting from the beeper on his belt. His hand moved smoothly to silence the sound.

Irritation flared silently in Tracy's chest. He thrived on it, the constant reminder of business. Just as her father had. ''That's one opinion.'' She laughed lightly, refusing to let her cynicism show.

''Meaning you have something against working?'' Clay teased. He turned off the highway onto a surface street that followed the shoreline and stopped at the curb, pointing to a telephone booth across the street.

''What's wrong with that?''

''You were born too late to be a flower child. Might as well face it. The work ethic is respectable again.'' Clay chuckled. As he turned the key the soft sound of the motor stopped, and the confined space inside the car seemed isolated from the surf and sunbathers and frolicking teenagers.

''If a little is good for you, a lot is better.'' Her voice changed against her will, erasing all evidence of the humor she'd tried so hard to maintain. ''Jump on the stress circuit. Never mind that you're a husband and father. Ignore warning signs. Divorce ahead. Heart attack around the next curve.''

She hadn't meant to look at him, and when she saw

the compassion in his eyes she wished she hadn't allowed herself to. She didn't want tenderness or understanding from him. She wanted him to be the Scrooge and evictor of widows she'd labeled him.

"It's not only overwork that causes divorce and illness," he said softly.

She caught her breath, aware he was speaking of his own father. She pulled her gaze away quickly, fearful that her eyes might soften with the sudden understanding. She looked over the sandy shore, focusing on the distant sea. Far beyond the surfers and swimmers, a sailboat skimmed gracefully on the surface of the sunlit water, and she watched it until she felt she could speak.

"I know. I forget sometimes that other people have pain." She kneaded the soft leather of her handbag. She was amazed that she could admit the fact. Once she had, she couldn't help admitting another fact. "But you don't seem bitter about it."

He took a deep breath of the ocean air while his gaze followed a jogger leaving footprints in the surf-sloshed sand. "I was for a while. I didn't want to leave the beach—this beach. But life goes on." He laughed with a little embarrassment. "As someone wiser once said." His gaze moved to a thin, bikini-clad girl attempting to upright a sailboat in the surf near the shore. "I made new friends in the East and looked forward to spending part of every summer in the West. Loafing, I guess you'd call it. But I thought it wonderful that Dad took off every day to play."

"I can't remember a time my father took off to play." Tracy hated the note of regret entering her voice. She'd steeled herself long ago against minding that other children went with their parents on picnics and trips to Sea World and Disneyland. If she went, it was with a girlfriend whose parents had invited her along. It wasn't the same. She'd wanted to invite someone to go with her and her parents sometimes. After her mother had left, she felt the other parents only asked her because they were sorry for her. And who wanted to be invited on an outing as an act of charity? Of course, going with Jolie was different. Jolie was two years younger, and Rose seemed delighted to have Tracy go with them to keep an eye on the active youngster. "I always thought there would be a time when my father would take off. I guess I was still hoping. . . . When he died, I was angry. He'd promised to attend my graduation—just as he'd promised to be at so many other events. So I just didn't graduate."

"And you haven't been able to forgive him." Clay's tone was neutral.

"Have you forgiven your father?" Tracy asked defensively.

"I didn't have to. Only when I was older did I realize the hotel and his health were going downhill faster than a surfer sliding down a fifty-foot wave." He sighed. "Even though my mother reminded me of his failings and faults as regularly as she watered her roses."

"She could have tried to change him."

"But she didn't love him anymore."

"You did."

"Somehow, my love accepts him . . . warts and all." He opened the car door quickly, as if embarrassed he'd talked so much. "I'll try not to take long with this call."

Tracy watched with a feeling of admiration as he strode confidently across the street. When he lifted the telephone receiver and stepped back so his hair gleamed in the sunlight, the admiration turned unexpectedly to a stronger feeling. She looked away.

It took a a moment to steady her thoughts. A moment to tamp down the chaotic feeling and tell herself she must leave before her heart overruled her head. As soon as Aunt Charli could cope with crutches or a walking cast, she was on her way back to Taos. But her head wasn't convinced.

She looked back at Clay. Her employer, Bryce, was so different. He had not one quick bone in his body, nor did he have a feverish desire to make money. He seldom rushed, whether waiting on customers in the art and craft shop, shaping his latest sculpture, or, for that matter, opening the shop on time. Who else would have said "Take all the time off you need" when she'd told him about her aunt's problems?

Tracy followed the outline of Clay's broad shoulders under the well-cut jacket. Yes, she assured herself, she looked forward to returning to the lackadaisical life in Taos. Not that Bryce was the one to share it with. But his presence was no threat to her life-style. She couldn't say that about her current escort.

Chapter Five

Tracy took a square of fudge from the candy case, nibbled off one corner, and placed the remainder on a piece of waxed paper. It must be noon. Her stomach felt as if she'd gone on a liquid diet, and her nerves were primed to growl at the next person who walked through the door. Her vision blurring, she lifted the cup of coffee she'd found cold an hour ago and assured herself one magical sip would paint a smile on her face for the customer who'd paused to speak to someone before entering the shop.

She'd awoken late, and the telephone had started ringing while she was measuring coffee beans for the grinder.

First, it was Sonjia apologizing for the early call but saying her daughter probably had strep throat and she had an appointment with the pediatrician. Tracy replied she hoped the child was better soon and replaced the receiver.

Before she'd started the coffee grinder, the telephone sounded again. This time, it was Madge calling to say she'd be late. The battery in her car was down. Tracy had dumped the beans back into the package and resealed the bag, consoling herself with the thought of the coffeepot at the shop.

But after calling to chat with Aunt Charli, she'd been late opening the shop and an irritable customer was waiting to buy chocolates for a party. Despite her impatience, it had taken the buyer half an hour to pick and choose truffles. Tracy had served a slow but steady stream of customers until Madge arrived near eleven, carrying a fast-food bag that emitted a delicious aroma.

Tracy moaned inwardly and tried to appease her stomach with chocolate. She broke off another thumbnail-sized piece of fudge from the square. Before she could pop it in her mouth, a new arrival barreled through the doorway and stopped with a huff before the counter.

Tracy lowered the candy and looked up to see a familiar face struggling to prevent a grin from overpowering her scowl. The wavering scowl disappeared about the time Tracy's childhood chum had one forefinger in motion.

"Fine friend you are," Joleen Gaynor admonished. "I've been calling you for two days. Anyone who is on the go as much as you are needs a cellular telephone."

Tracy lifted her eyes and opened her palms toward the ceiling. "Stand me in the corner . . . bury my feet in sand. . . ." She hurried around the counter to embrace her friend and then stood back, appraising her.

"You look wonderful. Must have a new man in your life that you didn't tell me about in your letters."

"Stop trying to evade the issue. How long have you been in town and how long are you going to stay?" Jolie clung to Tracy's hands.

"You mean your mother didn't tell you?" Tracy teased.

"She and Charli said something like you paid a surprise visit about the time Charli broke an ankle, and you only meant to stay the weekend but you were staying longer to help in the shop until Charli was up and about."

"That's about it."

"I'm sorry about Charli. But she seems in great spirits. Said you should get away from the shop for a while. So, I'm going to a patio party this evening—just some of the people we know who are still in the area—and I came to get you."

Tracy grimaced. "Wish I could come. But I can't leave the shop now."

"I'll pick you up. I don't want to go alone. You close at six, don't you?"

"Eight. But we have candy cases to refill before the weekend. Aunt Charli says that's one of our busiest times. Then I should visit Aunt Charli."

Madge's footsteps sounded on the tiles before she stepped from the kitchen, removing her chocolate-stained apron. "Thought you might like to go to lunch soon." She discarded the apron and replaced it with the dainty lace circle she wore behind the counter.

Tracy nodded at Madge. "I'll just grab a hot dog at that little shop down the street."

"You need a longer break than that," Madge admonished mildly.

"That's what I told her," Jolie said vehemently. "Sounds like she needs to take a break from the shop and her visiting nurse role."

"I don't spend all my time at the shop or with Aunt Charli," Tracy interjected.

"I know," Madge laughed. "You spend the rest of it trying to find a way to help Charli keep her shop in the hotel." She came around the counter and loosened the ties on Tracy's apron. "Go," she said humorously.

Jolie smiled at Madge gratefully. "Tell her spending an evening partying with old friends is also good for that frazzled look she's wearing. We've been invited to a patio party."

"Take her," Madge agreed enthusiastically. "Lindon will close the shop as usual and I'll call Charli."

"Meanwhile, let's go to lunch at the mall in Orange County," Jolie chortled.

Madge polished a print from the glass case. "Don't hurry back. Lindon will be here at one. You do look a bit tired and I expect we'll have a busy weekend from the looks of the weather."

Turning off the coast highway, Jolie turned her compact car inland to the mammoth shopping center. She guided the small car deftly into a marked parking space and switched off the ignition.

"Bring back memories?" Grinning, she loosened her seat belt.

"Like dressing in designer jeans and hanging out at

the mall on Saturdays pretending we didn't expect to be noticed.'' Tracy opened the car door and stepped onto the asphalt.

Jolie walked around the car to fall in step with Tracy as they walked toward the shopping center.

''Or spending an hour trying to decide what to have for lunch,'' Jolie said.

''Are the eating shops on the lower level still the same?'' Tracy asked eagerly.

''Maybe not the same as when we were teenagers,'' Jolie replied. ''But they are still there. Why do you think we came here?''

''If I remember, shopping may have something to do with it. You used to say you were only going to work to support your hobby.''

''I did better than that. My hobby is my work.''

''Tell me more.''

''I've been promoted to assistant buyer for a department store.''

''Oh, Jolie, that's great. Does this mean you get to go to New York or Paris for the fashion shows and that sort of thing?''

Jolie giggled. ''I wish.'' She tugged on Tracy's arm to stop her in front of a display window. A thin mannequin dressed in a midcalf-length spring green skirt with a matching scoop-necked blouse of the same delicate fabric gazed haughtily down at them. ''That would look gorgeous on you to wear to Mom and Dad's anniversary party.''

''Part-time work in an art shop doesn't pay that well.''

''A good reason to leave Taos and come back to California. I might even get you on where I work.''

"You too!" Tracy sighed dramatically.

"Me too what?" Jolie lifted her eyebrows. "All I said was that dress would look great to wear to an anniversary bash."

"All you said was to stop lollygagging in an art store and get to work." She shook her head in feigned exasperation. "It must be contagious . . . this preoccupation with success." Tracy strolled past the display window, speaking over her shoulder. "Which way to the food? I'm starving."

Jolie caught up with her and pointed the way to the escalator. Even before they reached the lower level, the sound of a pianist and the aroma of cooking left little doubt as to which way to turn.

Tracy stepped off the moving stairway, turning toward the cosily clustered chairs and tables surrounded by a variety of food booths.

"Chinese?" She looked at her friend and lifted an eyebrow.

"Appeals to me," Jolie said cheerfully.

After making their selections, Jolie pointed toward a refreshment booth and left Tracy to pick up their food. By the time Tracy had carried the food tray to an unoccupied table, Jolie approached with two glasses of sparkling water.

Jolie placed the glasses on the table, adeptly helped lift the food containers from the tray, and pushed paper-wrapped chopsticks toward Tracy. Sitting down, she took a sip of her drink before she lifted her gaze and smiled blandly at Tracy. "Now, tell me who's nagging you to work? Surely not Charli. I remember when she hung a GONE SHOPPING sign on the store in midafternoon."

Tracy looked at the chopsticks warily. "Could be why she may lose the shop," she said grimly. She unwrapped the wooden sticks, knowing her skill at using them was on a par with her painting ability. "That, and a landlord who's raising the rent so she can't afford to stay."

"You mean Clay Winter? Mother says he's done wonders with the hotel." Jolie lifted a sliver of chicken caught between two chopsticks. "Have you met him?"

Tracy lowered her eyes to examine the food on her plate and nodded.

"What do you think? Dreamy, huh?"

What did she think about him? Tracy stabbed at a shiny green pea pod. All she did lately was think about him, but she wasn't about to put her confused thoughts into words. "He's okay." She knew she sounded like a teenager denying she had a gigantic crush on a boy.

"Dreamy." Jolie repeated. "When I reach the point where I can call a man for a date, his number is the first one I'll punch in."

Narrowing her eyes, Tracy focused on the green pod, balancing it between the chopsticks. "If you want to talk about work all evening, he's a marvelous conversationalist."

"Aah," Jolie said with an air of understanding. "He's the one who has your dander up."

"He doesn't have my dander up." The pea slid from between the slivers of wood and plopped back on her plate.

"Couldn't tell it by the color of your cheeks."

Tracy stared at the plastic fork wistfully, and repositioned the sticks between her fingers. With determination, she prodded the elusive pod between the points and raised it carefully to her mouth. Chewing with satisfaction, she gazed toward the pianist as if enraptured by the familiar tune he played and searched her mind frantically for a topic unrelated to Clay Winter.

"I imagine Aunt Charli will be out of the hospital in time for the anniversary party, so you're right about a new dress. I didn't bring anything suitable to wear. I didn't know I'd be here that long. Maybe I should go back and try on that dress." She giggled. "Of course, Rose will think I'm a traitor if I buy anywhere but Chantilly Rose."

"Mom can probably order it for you." Jolie deftly lifted a cluster of noodles with her chopsticks. "The anniversary thing is being held in the Hibiscus Room at the hotel, you know."

"It is?" Tracy couldn't repress a feeling of pleasure. She could imagine Clay's eyes lighting up as she walked across the lobby in the gauzy green dress. Of course he'd see her. Wasn't he always at the hotel?

"Speaking of Clay Winter, he's been invited and he hasn't sent regrets." Jolie balanced a pink shrimp between her sticks and lifted it skillfully to her mouth. "Too bad I have a date. Guess you'll have to be kind to the poor man and see that he isn't bored." Her brown eyes lighted mischievously.

"I doubt if he ever gets bored," Tracy said wryly. "He's too busy." She looked up to see an approaching group of tourists, their name tags embellished with brightly colored logos. Chatting and laughing animatedly, they slid their food selections on the table. It made Tracy think of her tour of Italy. She hadn't gone without breakfast to get to work or gulped her lunch with one eye on her wristwatch. Or worried about the lack of chocolates in the display case.

Emptying her glass, Jolie raised an eyebrow at Tracy. "Are you ready to check out the shops? I'm mixing pleasure with business today."

Tracy feigned a groan. "Like someone else I know."

"I have to see what the competition is showing," she said cheerfully.

They strolled from one chic boutique to another and spent an hour in one department store. What was work for Jolie was relaxation for Tracy. It was four o'clock by the time she looked at her watch and insisted on returning to the candy shop. Sighing, Jolie searched for her car keys.

She stopped the car in front of the candy shop and waited for Tracy to disembark. "Remember, I'll pick you up at eight."

Tracy shook her head in mock frustration. "I don't have time to go to a party."

"You don't have time to go to a party?" Jolie's cheerful grin faded. "Every time you write, which isn't often, you rave about your carefree life."

Tracy winced at Joleen's crestfallen look. Fake or not, it still brought a wave of guilt. She sighed heavily, indicating her capitulation with a dramatic drop of her head. "What do I wear?"

Jolie smiled triumphantly. "You haven't been away that long," she admonished. "You know a California patio party. Anything from short shorts to an ankle-length muumuu."

"Eight. You know Aunt Charli's address?"

"Unless she's moved."

Tracy hesitated. "Maybe I should take a car. I do need to leave early."

"But you will be there."

Tracy crossed her heart, restraining a giggle as she nodded. Reluctantly, Jolie found a scrap of paper and wrote directions for their destination.

Tracy stood on the sidewalk and waved as Jolie drove away. She paused before entering the shop, viewing the multitude of people across the street. Mild weather had brought out senior citizens and shoppers to stroll the sunny sidewalks. Tomorrow, tourists and teenagers would increase the throng. What she needed was to lure more people into Aunt Charli's shop.

She pursed her lips. Strollers wouldn't raise the revenue. The real need was to lure conference attendees into the shop. A hundred or so people who needed to take home something to the wife and kids or girlfriends or boyfriends or secretaries. The caterer's business was in the future, if it worked out. The conference was next week, and they could sell a lot of candy. If she was a sharp businesswoman, she would capitalize on Clay's business acumen by courting the conference group. But she wasn't a sharp businesswoman. She sighed. She wasn't any kind of businesswoman. With her lack of experience, how did she think she could make a difference in the candy shop revenue in only a few weeks? Too much proximity to the charming CEO had her forgetting her adopted life-style, not to mention reaching for unattainable stars. She'd help in the shop and care for Aunt Charli and return to Taos in a few weeks. Wasn't that the wise thing to do?

It was almost five when she walked into the shop

and took over the counter from Madge. Business was unusually brisk, and she was surprised when Madge emerged from the back room, placed a tray of chocolates on the counter, and began untying her chocolate-splotched apron.

"Lindon got here just before you did—problem with his car, so we didn't get to the fudge." Madge eyed the depleted cases with a grimace. "Hope we have enough for tomorrow. I wouldn't leave, but I promised to sit with my sister's kids for the weekend. It's their anniversary." She removed the apron. "They seldom go out, and they've saved to rent a cabin in the mountains." She looked truly sorry. "Lindon doesn't work on Saturdays. His religion," she added. "But Sonjia called and she'll be here. Turned out her daughter just has a mild throat infection."

Tracy took the tray, her heart plummeting toward the tiles on the candy shop floor. Panic loomed just beyond the single layer of fudge squares on her far right. How could she face Saturday morning with a handful of fudge and part-time help? Turning away from Madge, she dipped her head and carefully layered the candy in the display case. She didn't even know how to run the shop for one day. Another reason to question her ability to help Aunt Charli increase her revenue!

Madge went around the counter and stopped in front of the display case. "Maybe I could get someone to sit with the kids and come in for a few hours tomorrow."

Tracy raised her head, tipped her chin upward, and smiled brightly at Madge. "Hey, no problem. If we don't find time to do the fudge tonight, I'll come in early tomorrow morning.''

An hour later, Tracy knew she had to keep her promise to Jolie. She might not stay late, but at least she'd be there for Jolie's sake.

Leaving Lindon in the shop, she looked toward the entrance to the hotel as she left and then mentally scolded herself. In the first place, she didn't want to see Clay. In the second place, there was little chance she would. Clay didn't leave work this early.

She called Aunt Charli as soon as she reached the condo, explaining why she wouldn't be by to visit. Charli assured her Rose and she were fine. "Go to the party and have a good time. Don't worry about the shop.''

But Tracy couldn't help worrying as she drove to the party.

At the party, despite the music and laughter and even a walk on the beach with a former high school beau, now in medical school, the thought of the un-made fudge nagged her. Finding Jolie, she explained about the fudge and endured a scowl. Then she found her hostess.

She stood before the shop at eleven. How could she sleep tonight, not knowing if Lindon had finished the chocolate? she asked herself.

Sliding the key in the lock of the door, she glanced involuntarily toward the lobby of the hotel. For a moment, she thought she saw Clay and her heartbeat quickened. Then the man moved farther into the lobby and she told herself she must be mistaken. It was wishful thinking. She turned the key and opened the door.

Switching on the overhead light in the kitchen, she nodded in silent approval at her decision to return. The fudge rested covered on the marble counter, but there was no sign of a new supply of chocolate-covered fudge balls.

She donned an apron and moved to the marble counter, thinking about the familiar figure in the lobby. Maybe Clay checking on the water in the plants or the shine on the tabletops, she thought wryly, and then laughed. Who was she to call the kettle black? It was nearing midnight and she'd left a perfectly good party to slave over a hot stove. She glanced at the microwave ovens and amended her phrase mentally.

She extracted a strip of fudge, her thoughts returning to Clay as her fingers formed golf ball–sized clumps of chocolate. Maybe he was concerned about the readiness of the hotel for the anticipated conference group. He had been excited about the prospective business. She lined chocolate balls on a tray. Maybe that's what she should be doing. Even without added effort, the increase in weekend guests could generate a lot of business for the shop. She rolled another ball, her mind racing.

As long as she was going to be here, she might do a little advertising for the shop. Maybe give free samples to the arriving guests.

However, sampling a freebie didn't mean they would look at the logo and connect it with the hotel candy shop. She needed a way to ensure they would come into Charli's Chocolates.

Separating another slab of chocolate, she mused

about printing fliers containing a coupon for a sample of Charli's wares. She could ask Clay for permission to put a flier in each guest room. She wrinkled her forehead. That meant seeing him again, and she had enough on her mind without worrying about protecting her heart.

High school students could distribute the fliers to guests as they arrived, her muse continued as if it hadn't been interrupted by thoughts of Clay.

Leaving the balls on a tray, she moved to the shelves and removed three packets of chocolate. She dumped part of a packet into a glass mixing bowl, placed it in a microwave oven, and set the timer. Glancing at the clumps she planned to dip in chocolate, she wondered if the chocolate-covered fudge balls were too expensive as samples. The timer sounded and she removed the bowl from the microwave to stir the melting mixture. Actually, she shouldn't fret about the cost. It was an advertising expense. The sample must be good enough to compel customers to buy. If the plan worked, Aunt Charli could try it on other occasions. She shoved the bowl back into the microwave and reset the time. By the time she returned to Taos, Aunt Charli should be at the shop with a slight increase in business. So why was she reluctant to think of leaving?

She was startled by a knock on the back door. Then she relaxed. It was probably Lindon coming back to work.

Wiping chocolate-stained fingers on her apron, she opened the door as far as the chain lock would allow. Expecting Lindon, fingers poised to release the chain, she stared at the friendly face outlined in the slat-thin opening with a quickening heartbeat.

"Saw the light on. Is it too late to talk business?"

Irritation at the word interrupted her elation at seeing Clay.

"Business?"

"Thought I'd stop by and place an order for the chocolate seashells." His smile was enchanting.

Business. She'd never thought she'd want Clay to mention that word, but this time it was different. Tracy took a deep breath. She couldn't remember which of his employees was supposed to go over the numbers, but she had to say something. She met his eyes through the narrow opening. "Your accountant approved?" She struggled to ask the question in a businesslike tone.

Clay hunched his shoulders, dipped his head, and pretended to shiver. "Do you think I could come inside? The fog is heavy enough to qualify as rain."

Embarrassed, Tracy fumbled with the lock, hope for her project building in her chest. By the time she had the door open, she was smiling.

"I hope you have good news."

"Would I bring bad news at this time of night?" He grinned. "Might spoil your dreams."

"Can we talk while I work?" She closed the door. Not waiting for an answer, she walked back to the worktable, motioned to a high stool nearby, and stepped to the microwave to remove the warmed bowl of dipping chocolate.

He ignored the seat, stopping at the end of the counter to lean one hip lightly against the rim of the marble top.

"I'd ask what you're doing here at this time of night, but it's pretty obvious. So I guess the next question is why?"

"Low inventory, absent employees." She moaned in frustration as a glob of chocolate slipped from her dipper, plopping into the bowl to splatter chocolate across the counter. "There goes Aunt Charli's profit," Tracy said wryly. "I waste more than I make."

"I wouldn't say it's wasted." Curling his fingers into his palm, Clay extended a forefinger and scooped the errant chocolate from the marble.

Tracy momentarily forgot to retrieve the fallen ball from the dipping bowl. Mesmerized, she watched his finger travel toward his lips. When he ran his tongue over his upper lip in dramatic anticipation, she almost caught her breath. Shaking herself mentally, she jabbed into the dipping chocolate.

"Delicious," Clay said. "Next splatter is for you."

Tracy smiled weakly and pulled the laden ball from the bowl. She lowered it carefully to the tray, giving herself time to compose her thoughts.

"Did your accountant like my figures?" She grimaced. "That didn't come out just right."

Clay nodded, reaching to pull the chair to the end of the counter. He sat down. "Anything I can do to help?"

"Not right now." Tracy managed to hang on to a hair of patience. If there was a problem, why didn't he say so? "He just hopes you can keep up with the demand."

Tracy kept her face immobile as she resumed her work. Clay would pick tonight to bring her the news. She knew she was inept at candymaking. Having Clay sitting close enough for his aftershave to overpower the aroma of chocolate didn't help.

She dipped the last ball into the bowl. "Aunt Charli will be back in the shop soon. If she can't rehire her old help, she can train new ones."

She lifted the ball, transferred it to the tray, and lifted a hand to brush her knuckles across her cheek.

"Working this late is unusual. You know, with people out sick and inexperienced help like me." She laughed weakly.

"That was his comment, not mine. I have no doubt you, uh, Charli's Chocolates can come through. We just wanted to let you know we expect things to start looking up." He nodded at the filled tray. "Can I put that somewhere for you?"

Tracy nodded, indicating the cooling shelf. She gathered the bowls and utensils and carried them to the sink. Turning on the tap, she caught a familiar scent.

"Tea towel?" Clay queried.

"I can leave the dishes draining," Tracy protested. She needed him out of her space, she told herself. His smell, his body, and his sensuous lips.

"Nonsense. The sooner we're finished, the sooner we can find someplace to serve us a late snack."

"I'm too beat to go out." She scrubbed at caked chocolate.

"That's why you should tell me where to find a towel. A cup of cappuccino, decaf of course, is good for that 'beat' feeling."

Laughing in resignation, Tracy waved a soapy hand toward a nearby shelf. "I don't pay volunteer help, you know."

"Perks are enough for me," Clay responded. He rolled his eyes toward the chocolate-laden shelves.

With the dishes out of sight, Tracy rotated her shoulders and turned to lean against the sink, her eyes scanning the area to ensure its readiness for the morning work.

Clay moved to stand in front of her, his eyes roaming over her face with an unbusinesslike look.

"I doubt if chocolate rouge is the latest trend, even for a midnight coffee break."

He raised his hand and touched her face with the damp cloth, moving it gently, like a caress across her cheek, then pausing for a moment to inspect her face for further evidence of her fingers' travels.

Butterflies swarmed in her stomach. She knew she should laugh and make a light, witty remark and then move away in search of an unavailable sweater against the slight chill of the sea air. But her feet stuck to the tiles as if she'd stepped in globs of congealing chocolate. Why was it a surprise to find her wits had deserted her again?

"One more spot." He raised a finger to her lower lip and drew it across the sensitive skin. "Of course, that's not the best way to remove chocolate stains." His voice was hoarse. His lips lowered to cover hers gently.

She closed her eyes, feeling the pleasure of his touch warm her, and then she felt his lips move away and she opened her eyes to gaze into his.

"I've wanted to hold you since the first time I met you in that crowd in the Hibiscus Room." His hand moved across her cheek and paused at the corner of her mouth. "I have trouble keeping my mind on business when I'm in the office and trouble keeping my mind on sleeping when I'm in bed. Would you say I had a problem?''

Tracy held her breath. The confident, almost arrogant CEO of Winter's Inn was admitting a weakness for which he held her responsible. The thought was more unnerving than she could have imagined.

As if she had no willpower, her right hand slid around his neck, her fingers moving to twine through his hair. What was she doing? she asked herself and stilled the fingers. But she couldn't move them away. The smooth, silken strands were like a snare. She tilted her head and raised her lips to his, and the unspoken invitation was accepted. She savored the warmth of his lips until her head reeled. Vaguely, she felt a pounding against her rib cage, like incoming surf on a rocky shore, and took it as a warning. To give her heart to a workaholic was no better than letting it crash against the rocks and lie battered and bruised in the outgoing surf.

Slowly, she pulled away and slid her hands down, resting the palms on his chest.

''I'd say your problem is no worse than mine. But it'll go away.'' Her voice was light. She stepped back. ''Are we going out for cappuccino or what? I have to get up early in the morning.''

''That's all?'' Clay's voice strained for humor. ''I admit you're more important than business and you tell me you have to get up early to work tomorrow. What happened to the carefree life?''

''So I've changed. For the time being,'' she amended. Heart pounding in a rush that made her dizzy, she walked carefully to retrieve her purse.

"There's hope for you." His voice followed her.

But is there for you? she wondered as she turned and walked back to him with a smile. She pulled the door closed behind them and felt an irresistible surge of pleasure as he took her hand and looped it through his bent arm. Smiling, she walked toward the hotel. She'd worry tomorrow about putting the fences back around her heart.

Chapter Six

With an outlook as bright as the midday sun, Tracy left the shop for a lunch break Saturday, using evasive tactics to wend a path through the crowded walkways. Teenagers roamed the sidewalks in exuberant packs, parting like the Red Sea to allow hand-holding lovers to pass. Weekend tourists shuffled along, grinning with amiable tolerance at the teenagers, and shopping mothers kept a frustrated but keen watch over straying toddlers.

Grateful for a respite from the busy shop, Tracy made her way to a bench with a view of the ocean. As usual, it was occupied. As was the one on the other side of the walkway. But there was room for one more person. She smiled at the older couple enjoying the view and sat on one end of the slatted bench.

Unwrapping her pita sandwich, she watched a de-livery girl from the flower shop struggling to keep a bouquet of helium-filled balloons from escaping her grasp. The colorful Mylar and latex balls dipped and danced in the ocean breeze, adding to Tracy's feeling of well-being. She found herself smiling at the slightest thing. The stream of customers into the shop had been steady, keeping her mind off Clay, but now that she was alone she couldn't help thinking of him. Each time her head reminded her he was a workaholic, her heart said so what. The feelings Clay had left her with last night still lingered.

She wondered where he was today. He hadn't mentioned a meeting or an out-of-town conference, but she hadn't seen him enter the hotel. Dreamily, she nibbled at the sandwich. It was difficult to force herself to finish it and more difficult to return to work.

She left the shop at seven-thirty, anxious to call Aunt Charli about the extra income. On the way to the car, she decided to visit her aunt at Rose's instead.

She drove up the winding road that led to the Gaynors' hilltop home and parked in the circular drive beside a faintly familiar car. Only when she rang the doorbell did she recall who owned the car. A minute later, the owner stood in the doorway.

The words on the tip of her tongue died under the onslaught of a suddenly racing heart.

Her appearance seemed to have the same effect on Clay, but his recovery was faster.

"Hi, Tracy. Glad you're here. I was just leaving."

He grinned. "I didn't mean that like it sounded. I meant I met Rose at the gas station a little while ago. She was on her way to the airport to pick up Martin and was worried about leaving Charli, so I told her I was going this way and I'd stop by."

Tracy grinned even broader. "Just going by this way?" She waved at the expanse of curving road below.

"I meant to get to the hospital again and didn't. So I wanted to see Charli."

"Don't leave. I want to tell Aunt Charli about the additional revenue for the store." She smiled. "I couldn't have done it without you."

He shrugged lightly. "You had something the hotel could use, and you presented it in such a way I couldn't refuse."

Clay stepped back for Tracy to enter and followed her to the broad veranda overlooking the ocean, where Charli sat in a cushioned lounge chair.

Charli greeted her niece and tapped the book in her hand with a lacquered nail before placing it on a nearby table. "The blurb on the back cover reads well. Thanks for thinking of me."

Clay nodded in acknowledgement and waited for Tracy to choose a chair. When Tracy lifted her head, Charli was looking from her to Clay with a pleased look. Clay's look was just as smug, as if they shared a common thought.

"What have you and Clay been doing at the hotel while I've been tied to this unwieldy contraption?" Charli glanced at her cast disdainfully.

"Clay and I haven't been doing anything...." Tracy felt her tongue tangle. Why could she speak the English language quite well except when Clay was near?

"I mean, we've been doing something, but not together. Not exactly together." Words tumbled out like popcorn spilling from a popper.

She started over, focusing her eyes on her aunt. "I know you've been worried about the increase in the rent on the shop, and Clay mentioned the shopkeepers should get new business just as he is getting hotel guests." She paused for a breath. "So I came up with a scheme to supply the hotel with chocolate treats from your shop."

She took another breath, her confidence returning, and grinned mischievously at Clay. "I figured I had one thing going for me. If you didn't help Aunt Charli increase her sales, you'd lose a renter. If you lost a renter, you'd be losing money all the time it took you to lease the shop again. Plus the expense of remodeling the space suitably for the next occupant."

Clay shook his head in amusement. "Who gave you the idea you couldn't be a businesswoman?"

"One idea doesn't make me a businesswoman."

"It's a start." Clay's eyes gleamed with approval. "If Charli doesn't have a place on her staff for you, I'm sure I can find one on mine."

Tracy threw up her hands in mock exasperation and laughed, turning to her aunt. "It's not enough that he's a workaholic. He tries to enlist anyone near him."

Charli chuckled. "When you two get through the mutual admiration bit, you might clue the chairman of the board in on this windfall destined for the shop."

Tracy turned back to her aunt, trying to concentrate on the answer. It wasn't easy with Clay sitting close enough to send a subtle scent of aftershave her way as well as radiate heat waves the sea breeze couldn't cool.

"Remember those gold-colored nets filled with chocolate seashells?" She paused as Aunt Charli nodded. "Well," she stuttered, worried, now, that she'd stepped on Aunt Charli's toes. "When I came to visit a few days ago, you were sleeping. . . . I was worried because you were concerned about money, and I'd had breakfast with Clay and his father and Clay seemed adamant about raising your rent."

She stopped herself from looking at the CEO. "I told you about my idea. To sell those seashells to the hotel for bedtime treats."

Aunt Charli nodded. "I thought it was a good idea."

"That's what you said. But you were groggy, and I was afraid you hadn't really listened."

Aunt Charli tilted her head and raised her eyes. "Anything connected with the shop breaks through all sound barriers. Of course I heard you. But if you thought I was trying to push you, you'd have been on the next plane to Taos."

"Aunt Charli," Tracy scolded mildly. "I wouldn't have left you in a hospital bed."

"If that's a promise, maybe I can rent one for a few years."

"That'll be the day. We'll be lucky to keep you in a wheelchair."

Clay entered the conversation, teasing Charli he'd help her with any plan to keep Tracy in Costa Corona. Laughter rippled over the veranda.

A fresh breeze rustled a potted Kentia palm and the soft, musical clang of seashell wind chimes sounded across the veranda. Clay rose as if the visiting bell in a hospital had sounded.

Tracy looked up, a sense of disappointment dulling

the echo of the laughter. "Visiting hours aren't over," she said lightly.

"They are for me," Clay said. His face settled in a mournful look momentarily. "I have a dinner engagement."

Tracy felt more mournful than he looked and thought of the chesty, leggy lady posing with Clay at the preopening cocktail party.

"Business engagement," Clay added.

The sudden despair disappeared as swiftly as it had come. Tracy stood, waiting for Clay to say good night to her aunt before she accompanied him to the door.

"I haven't told her about my idea for next weekend." Tracy opened the door and followed Clay to the porch.

Clay turned and faced her. "Next weekend?"

"The conference group you are expecting. I thought I'd give coupons for free samples to all the guests as they arrive. Later on they might drop into the shop to make a purchase."

"Sounds good. But check-in time is pretty hectic."

"I don't mean inside the hotel. I'd have the distributors outside, catching guests as they entered." She paused, hoping the explanation sounded plausible. "I thought if we waited, we might catch the same people over and over and never see those again who don't leave the hotel. Some conference people are too busy to leave the hotel once they check in."

His smile radiated to his eyes. "Sounds good. Between the coupons and the Charli's Chocolates emblem on the evening treat, you've got advertising covered for the weekend. You're a quick study."

For a moment, Tracy was startled into silence. The

look and words tugged at her senses, sending them soaring like helium-filled balloons tethered by colorful strips of ribbon.

With effort, she forced her feelings back to reality. She didn't want his praise. She didn't want the look that produced a glow in her, stunning her senses. She wanted him to see that Aunt Charli could keep the shop going.

"Thank you." Her smile was as demure as that of a Victorian debutante. *You're feeling gratitude,* she chided herself. *He's helping you to help Aunt Charli and you're mistaking it for love.* But it wasn't gratitude that had compelled her lips to search for his in the candy kitchen at midnight, was it?

"It's a lot of work." Clay's word's rang with a teasing, humorous tone. "You may be longing for the next flight to Taos before the conventioneers get here."

"I think I can handle it," Tracy said briskly.

Watching Clay's car wind down the road, she felt less confident than she had sounded. She had to keep not only her heart under control, but the upcoming project as well. The last time she'd had too many problems she'd fled to Italy. She wondered if Clay thought she'd flee to Taos in the same way, and then she realized Clay didn't know she'd cut classes, lost her fiancé, and gone to Italy to visit her wandering mother and stepfather after her father had died.

She wondered about the truth behind Clay's teasing words. Could she stick with the store if the going got rough?

* * *

Unable to sleep, Tracy riffled through the yellow pages, looking for printers and jotting down phone numbers. She could make a master copy of the advertisement. She'd had some experience in a class in college. She'd need to check the cost of printing against copying, though using a copy machine might be faster. It would be Monday before she could contact a printer.

Tracy arose early, even though the shop wasn't opened for business until noon on Sundays, anxious to start on the fliers. Reaching for the coffee carafe, she thought of Clay. Starting the coffee, she put bread in the toaster and wondered if Clay was having breakfast at the hotel. Even in the shower, the memory of his show of admiration at her new project sent waves of warmth through her as pleasurable as the tepid spray sliding off her skin.

Scrubbing her legs dry, she wrapped the towel around her, sarong style, and padded to the kitchen. She'd call Aunt Charli first, tell her about the plan, and then go to the shop. If she kept to a schedule . . . She didn't finish the thought. She'd stopped keeping schedules almost two years ago. The thought of Clay flashed in her mind, and she made a wry face. It was his fault. His subtle suggestions were a way of trying to change her life-style and she had no intention of succumbing. Well, maybe this once. She'd do the weekend conference thing to show him she wasn't a quitter. Not to mention the prime reason, she amended. If the coupon giveaway was a success, Aunt Charli could repeat it. Dressing quickly, she went to the kitchen.

She'd had only a few sips of coffee when the telephone rang.

Aunt Charli wanted to come home.

Tracy felt both frustrated and relieved. Frustrated at the delay in her plans for the morning and relieved that Aunt Charli was ready to come home. She banished the frustration. She was here to help Aunt Charli, she reminded herself. She was startled that she'd thought of the business first.

Humor overcame the momentary flash of irritation as she drove as fast as traffic along the coast highway would allow. She was doing it again. Clay would be elated. She was worrying about work. She lightened the pressure on the gas pedal and loosened her tense grip on the steering wheel. Where was her carefully cultivated "if you don't get it done today, you can get it done tomorrow" attitude? With an effort, she relaxed her shoulders and darted a glance at the ocean. A sleek white cabin cruiser glided over the morning sea. On the beach, treasure hunters, some with headphones like earmuffs, slid their metal detectors across the sand in search of buried loot. She should be on the beach seeking nothing more than elusive coins and a suntan, Tracy chided herself. She nodded as if to reinforce the thought. Knowing Aunt Charli, she'd be back in the shop tomorrow. Passing the new project along to her didn't sound illogical. Tomorrow afternoon she'd hit the beach. Maybe every afternoon. Seeing less of the shop and Clay was necessary to revitalize her.

Between visiting with Rose and Martin and their insistence she stay for lunch, it was almost two o'clock before Tracy had Charli seated in the car.

"I should go by and see if Lindon needs help," Tracy said.

"Good," Charli agreed enthusiastically. "I want to see the shop anyway."

"Seeing" the shop took up the afternoon.

Hours later, Tracy settled Aunt Charli in front of the television set, switched on the six o'clock news, and gave a fleeting thought to the contents of the refrigerator and cupboards.

Changing into shorts and a T-shirt, she grinned at Aunt Charli as she passed by on her way to the kitchen. Warily, she pulled open the refrigerator door. Not that she expected to see a ready-to-pop-in-the-oven casserole, but on the off chance that she'd overlooked a gift package of cheese and beef logs. Or a canned ham. She'd only opened it for milk and margarine so far. Sustenance came from drive-throughs, didn't it? Except maybe breakfast. She knew the dishwasher contained three or four rinsed cereal bowls.

She stared at the once–cream-colored chunk of Monterey Jack cheese now swathed in a velvety grayish green cloak that didn't enhance its appeal. The fleeting thought of exhibiting her few culinary skills to her aunt faded.

Strolling back to the living room with a tea towel draped over her left arm, she stood beside her aunt until Charli looked away from the television set.

"My name is Tracy," she said, struggling to control her laughter. "I'll be your waitress for this evening." She cleared her throat pretentiously. "Our specialties today are hamburgers from Burger Baron, Chinese from Flaming Dragon, tacos from Casa Maria, barbecued chicken." She paused, laughing. "I can't remember the name of the place, but I know where it is. We also have deep-fried fish and, uh, submarines.''

Charli's delight mingled with Tracy's. ''I see you've taken my 'shop locally' motto to heart.''

''Clay says I'm a fast learner.'' *Why,* she asked herself as the words spilled from her mouth before she could stop them, *did I think of Clay?* Embarrassed, she grinned at Aunt Charli.

Charli lifted an eyebrow. ''That's a nice compliment from a young man who had to learn how to turn the finances of Winter's Inn around in a few short years.'' She punched a button on the remote control, changing the channel on the television set as if changing the subject of conversation. ''How about fish this evening? I don't like the coleslaw at the fish place— too much mayonnaise—but the deli two blocks from the shop makes a great dish. Their potatoes are better too.''

Still recovering from her inadvertent reference to Clay, Tracy sighed. Neither place was a drive-through. Giving her shorts a cursory glance, she tugged the oversize T-shirt over her slender hips and decided she was too tired to change. Besides, she didn't know many people in Costa Corona.

Fifteen minutes later, arms loaded with food containers, she decided she knew one too many. Clay held the deli door open for her, his mischievous eyes giving her bare legs more than a cursory glance.

''It didn't take you long to find the best deli in town.'' His bulk took up half the doorway. ''Which is your favorite here, the German potato salad or the coleslaw?''

''Aunt Charli's favorite is the coleslaw. At least,

that's what she sent me to buy.'' She lowered her gaze to his chest. Just how did he expect her to get through the open door without brushing past him? She shifted the boxes and prepared to leave the shop. It was a challenge, but she was up to it.

''Thanks for gettin' the door.'' She pressed one side against the frame and slid past.

''My pleasure.'' Clay held the door open for an elderly couple and then caught up with her. ''Let me hold the food while you open the car door.'' He took the containers from her hands without waiting for an answer.

Waiting until she was inside the car, he handed her the food and closed the door.

Tracy tilted her chin to look up at him, fighting to keep her voice light. ''My aunt thanks you, I thank you. . . .''

''Again, my pleasure.'' Clay leaned forward and briefly placed his lips against hers.

Tracy's carefully maintained poise wavered. She felt as if she was riding a surfboard on a tidal wave. A solid surface of sand awaited her on a distant beach, but it wasn't visible now, let alone attainable. She struggled for control. If she didn't stop connecting with the magnetic gaze of Clay Winter, she would lose her balance and topple into a maelstrom that could change her way of life beyond recognition. It was a matter of survival. She forced the surfboard to calmer waters. ''Have to run before the coleslaw wilts,'' she said with forced gaiety. She drove away from the parking lot as if a giant wave threatened again.

* * *

On Monday, she was waiting for the print shop to open. It took less than ten minutes to find she could rent a computer by the hour, design her own flier, buy paper, and have the printer run it off for one cent less than it would cost to use the copy machine and use the shop's paper. She liked the idea of buying her own paper, toying with a choice of scarlet and silver, like Charli's logo. Worrying about the silver print, she chose strawberry- and lemon-colored paper. Black print would go well on both. As would Charli's logo. Nodding to the manager, she made her way to a computer and hoped she remembered something from her college class.

Four days later, with reams of fliers at her feet, Tracy explained the distribution plan to her teenage distributors.

At six o'clock that evening, she wondered if they had misunderstood. The weekenders should have checked in by now. She scanned the door of the sweet shop with rising anxiety. One lonely coupon rested in the walnut-stained basket near the cash register.

She looked up from waiting on an elderly woman to bid Lindon good night and told him to leave the OPEN sign in the window. With the hour hand on the clock slipping past eight, only three coupons had made their way to the candy counter.

At nine, Madge called. "You're still at the shop," she scolded.

"Just closing," Tracy said, wondering why she felt guilty.

"I wanted to assure you the flu bug has been eradicated and I'll be in to work tomorrow."

"I hope we have more business tomorrow than we're doing this evening. I stayed open late hoping some of the hotel guests would stop by after going out to dinner, but no one seems to be pampering their sweet tooth today."

"Speaking of working late," Madge said emphatically, "I called Charli's house first. Thought you'd be there. Charli said she expected you an hour ago. She's dressed and waiting to go to the Gaynors' anniversary party."

Tracy gasped. How could she have forgotten the Gaynors' anniversary party was this evening?

"I was just leaving," she stuttered.

"I would hope so," Madge said dryly. "You can't work all the time."

Tracy felt the words echoing in her mind. Madge was right. What was she doing here? It was against her principles. She brought her attention back to Madge's voice.

"You may have a late night," Madge continued. "Take the afternoon shift tomorrow. I doubt if many hotel guests will rise at nine to buy chocolates."

Tracy laughed wryly. "Be it nine in the morning or nine at night, I hope those coupons steer them into the shop sometime before they leave." She sighed heavily. "The teenagers will be at the shop at nine for a new load of fliers. Tell them not to miss anyone near the hotel tomorrow."

"Right," Madge affirmed. "I'll motivate them."

Replacing the receiver, Tracy walked over to switch off the overhead lights. Without warning, a rush of elation swept over her. She'd not only forgotten the anniversary party, she'd forgotten Clay had promised to be there.

She'd met him for coffee on Tuesday and he'd mentioned the Hibiscus Room was being readied for the Gaynors' party. When she'd told him she was taking Aunt Charli, he'd asked her to save a dance for him. "I may be late," he'd said. "I have to pick up a member of the hotel board at John Wayne Airport, but I'll be there to claim my dance."

With Aunt Charli impatiently drumming her fingertips, Tracy reached into the closet for the delicate celadon green dress she'd first seen while shopping with Jolie. As Jolie had suggested, she'd found Rose could also order it for her. She added gold-and-bronze sandals, elongated green-and-silver earrings, and a touch of lipstick as pale as the inner curve of a conch shell she'd bought to decorate the tiny table in the shop. Her hand quivered as she dabbed cologne on the hollow of her neck and her wrists. She was as anxious to reach the Hibiscus Room as Charli was.

The sound of music met Tracy as she pushed Aunt Charli's wheelchair into the crowded Hibiscus Room. The chandeliers gleamed in full glory, each polished cut of glass radiating flashes of light on the sequins and silks of the minglers and dancers below. Holding the wheelchair still, Tracy scanned the room, searching for the one face that had been in her thoughts. She didn't locate it.

Quelling her disappointment, she caught Jolie's eye, smiled broadly, and threaded Aunt Charli's chair through a narrow path to Rose and her husband. She found a comfortable spot for the chair. After bringing her aunt refreshments, she chatted with Jolie and her friend and then accepted an invitation to dance with the attractive man. She accepted a second invitation from an old acquaintance and laughed at his jokes. And all the time, she darted fleeting glances at the entrance to the room.

When Clay arrived, her heart thumped as if she hadn't expected his appearance. Keeping her feet in rhythm to the music, she turned her head to watch him, and his gaze lifted to look across the room. A smile spread across his face and the accompanying sparkle in his eyes left little doubt that it was meant for Tracy. Tracy felt her heart would crowd out all the air from her lungs.

Her partner told another joke and she laughed politely, wishing Clay would stride across the room and claim his dance. But he only nodded and turned away, and Tracy saw he was with someone. He introduced the distinguished-looking man to the honorees and then moved him to a nearby group. The music stopped. Tracy's dance partner guided her back toward Jolie, and then suddenly Clay encircled her waist with his arm and pulled her away.

"Don't tell me the band is on a break!" he wailed in mock distress. "I came to claim a dance with the prettiest woman in the room."

Tracy was unable to stop beaming. "With all your publicity expertise and advertising resources, you couldn't come up with a better line than that old cliché?"

"Not old, well-seasoned. And it's true." His warm voice made her forget the disappointment she'd felt on her arrival. It didn't matter that he was late. He was here. His arm was still around her waist, as if willing the band to start again.

The music started and Clay took her right hand, closing his fingers over the smooth skin. His other hand pulled her close. Slowly, she relaxed, and the arm she'd rested lightly on his shoulder moved so her hand touched the collar of his shirt. In return, his fingers moved softly along her back, sending a shiver of excitement to her toes. Her feet felt unusually agile, as if the sandals had been touched with magic, matching the graceful steps of her partner.

The music ended, and without releasing his hold, Clay bent his head down and looked at her, the endearing sparkle in his eyes radiating into hers.

"I faintly remember a song with a line like 'We could have danced all night.' I wish it could be true, but duty calls." He tilted his head toward the guest he'd left talking to the hostess.

Tracy's heart sank. "You warned me," she said lightly. She walked across the room with him and watched him leave, knowing the warning hadn't helped. She looked away. This was how it would always be with him. Work came first. Her mother's complaints came back to her. With a husband who was always at the office or with a client or poring over papers, her mother's social life had been as limited as their family life.

Her father's untimely death reinforced her fear of workaholics. Even if Clay managed to make it home for the occasional evening meal, she would always be worried that his stressful life-style would take him away from her.

She'd schooled her heart not to soften at the sight

of any man who resembled her father. She wanted a home life surrounded by knee-hugging children with their menagerie of dogs, pet rabbits, neon-colored fish, and crested cockatoos. Even a weed-choked lawn was included in her dream. But she wanted a nine-to-five husband to mow it while she cooked dinner.

Clay moved through the doorway and Tracy swallowed the lump building in her throat. She couldn't love a workaholic. She couldn't! But she did.

Chapter Seven

Tracy opened her eyes and grimaced. By the looks of the light streaming through a crooked venetian blind slat, she'd overslept.

She and Aunt Charli had arrived home well after midnight, and Aunt Charli had insisted she sleep late, saying Madge and Sonjia could handle the morning trade. Tracy hadn't argued, but she hadn't meant to do as her aunt suggested. Today was the big day. Those teenage distributors would be out there pushing fliers into the hands of everyone who even looked like they were entering the lobby of Winter's Inn, if she was any judge of Madge's enthusiasm for the project. Surely all of them wouldn't be tossed in the nearest trash container.

Slipping a robe over her short gown, she padded barefoot to the kitchen to find Aunt Charli struggling to reach the toaster. She knew she wasn't going to leave the apartment with a cup of coffee in hand. She greeted her aunt and opened the refrigerator resignedly.

Nor was she able to dash to the shop after their breakfast. Half a dozen other tasks took up the remainder of the morning. More than once, her hand reached for the telephone to ring Madge and see if she and Sonjia needed help. She hoped they did!

It hadn't been easy convincing Charli to rest another few days, and that she'd really be needed in the kitchen if their coupon lure worked. After dumping the dishes haphazardly in the dishwasher, Tracy dropped tea bags into a sun tea jar and placed an assortment of snacks within reach, called a neighbor to ensure she'd check with Charli periodically, and hurried to dress.

She looked over her scant wardrobe quickly, rejecting the jeans and T-shirts. It was a special day and she planned to stay behind the counter this afternoon. She pulled out the midcalf-length tiered skirt, a loose blouse, and the well-worn, comfortable sandals. Thinking of Clay, she took time to dab cologne on her neck and wrists, though she reasoned no one would be able to smell it over the aroma of chocolate.

Backing Charli's car from the garage, she waited for passing traffic, then pulled into the street and headed for the coast highway. Eager to reach the shop, she chafed at the usual snail-paced weekend traffic. Then, as the line of cars approached the hotel, she relaxed. The delay gave her a chance to scrutinize the sidewalk traffic, which seemed heavier than usual.

Momentarily, traffic stopped for a car to turn into the driveway entrance to the lobby and Tracy peered anxiously at the sidewalk. There was a long line of people in front of the hotel, ending at the door of the chocolate shop.

Tracy grinned ecstatically. Success. Madge's morning speech must have inspired the coupon distributors. A short beep from behind brought her attention back to the car, and she pressed on the pedal and moved with the traffic. Parking the car in the hotel lot, she walked briskly back to the shop.

Tracy wove past a jostling crowd to reach the door. She halted at the doorway, where two teenagers stood firmly blocking the opening. A tanned, grinning sixteen-year-old looked at her briefly before he extended a thumb in the direction she'd just come from.

"Line forms back there," he said cheerfully.

"I work here," Tracy said, matching his grin.

"Great," the youth exclaimed. "They need help inside. This line is slower than a turtle." He reached to the youths in the doorway. "Hey, make way for the hired help."

Relaying the message to the people inside, the young men stepped back. Then they bowed with a wide sweep of their bare, sun-bronzed arms to wave Tracy on. Caught up in the jovial atmosphere, Tracy nodded to each youth and went through the doorway. She moved behind the counter, stashing her purse on a shelf and ignoring the lacy apron. She glanced at the sea of faces partly obscured by the waving fliers.

"It's been this way since ten o'clock," Madge said with a hint of weariness. She turned to pass a chocolate sample to a spike-haired teenager.

"They look young for convention attendees," Tracy commented.

"They're not buying, either," Sonjia whispered.

Laughter echoed from the doorway and Tracy glanced outside. Two tall teenagers good-naturedly jockeyed for a position in the line. Tracy caught her breath. She doubted if Clay would approve of the exuberant young people, who broke their line only to allow cars to enter the covered drive. A disturbance was the last thing she needed.

Tracy pushed her way to the doorway, pasting a grin on her face that she hoped was a crowd controller. By the time she reached the door, the disturbance had subsided. She breathed a sigh of relief. Then she looked down the line. The jostling, cheerful line had flowed across the drive and a frustrated doorman was trying valiantly to wave the young people aside to allow a car to enter the driveway. Anxiety building, Tracy hurried toward the chaotic scene.

Without warning, she felt a firm hand clamp her arm. "What's going on, Tracy?" Clay's voice was cool.

Tracy turned. He was dressed casually, in a navy blazer and gray trousers, and he looked wonderful. "I just got here," Tracy stammered.

Clay looked at her with an unreadable expression, then turned to one of the teenagers in line and asked the same question.

The teenager waved a flier. "Some guy on the beach is passing out these coupons for free chocolate."

Tracy's heart dropped to the sidewalk. Had the distributors interpreted Madge's instructions to include everyone within walking distance of the shop?

She glanced at Clay helplessly. "I only meant the coupons to be given to your hotel guests."

Clay nodded soberly, handed the flier back to the teenager, and assessed the lengthy line.

Tracy bit her lower lip, staring at his sober face. *Say it,* she said silently. *Go ahead and say I should have been here to see that my instructions were carried out.*

"I . . . I never expected this kind of response," she said instead.

Clay didn't smile. "Since it's happened, let's see if we can do something about it. I'll send some hotel personnel to help. Maybe they can take a supply of chocolate and go along the sidewalk exchanging it for the coupons." He paused, scanning the crowd, and waved at the nearest flier. "Do you know how many of these things have been passed out?"

Before Tracy could answer, the crowd broke into an excited chatter and people turned to look toward the hotel lobby.

Clay's head jerked around. "What now?" He turned abruptly and strode through the parting crowd toward the lobby.

Breaking into a run, Tracy followed. A giant compressor closed around her heart. *No,* she screamed silently. *Don't let it be one of the young people attacking a hotel guest.*

Three steps behind Clay, she saw him wave off a security guard and reach out to grasp a youth kneeling over a gray-haired man. Before he could yank up the youth, a second youth yelled at him.

"Hey, don't break the rhythm, man." The first youth lowered his head over the prone body again.

Clay's hand halted in midair, his eyes assessing the

scene in front of him. He straightened slowly and looked at the security guard.

"CPR," the guard said succinctly. "The man's wife"—the guard indicated a distraught woman nearby—"says he has a history of heart trouble. We've called an ambulance." ·He looked at his boss for approval. "These kids seem to know what they're doing."

Clay nodded and moved back. "See if you can get this crowd to give the boys some room." He moved to the distraught wife and bent toward her with concern in his hazel eyes.

Despite her anxiety, Tracy couldn't help but admire the way he cradled the woman's elbow in his calm, capable hand and guided her to a lounge chair. She couldn't hear the words, but she could see his sculpted lips moving and then giving a faint smile of reassurance to the woman. The woman responded with a choking sigh and gazed blindly toward the throng in front of her.

Tracy looked away, peering at the lingering crowd. Hotel guests and bystanders, some clad in colorful shorts or casual slacks, others dressed in business suits and spring dresses, milled in the lobby. Some gazed with unabashed curiosity at the ongoing drama in the middle of the room; others showed a tinge of frustration at their inability to get to their rooms. Tracy looked toward the revolving entry with trepidation. To her relief, it wasn't filled with departing guests. She forced air into her constricted lungs. She had only wanted to increase Charli's business before she returned to Taos. She hadn't meant to start a near riot or cause some elderly man to have a heart attack. She gazed back toward the lobby and saw the crowd parting. She caught a fleeting glance of the prone man on the carpet and the two young men bent over him. Then two paramedics moved through the parting crowd. She allowed herself another breath and looked toward Clay and the distraught wife.

She should have been here to see that everything went smoothly. She shouldn't have stayed out so late, she shouldn't have slept so late. . . .

Peering between two casually dressed people, Tracy could see one paramedic starting an intravenous line into the arm of the patient while the other attached monitor leads to his bared chest. The legs and torsos in front of her shifted, blocking her view of the patient, and she strained to hear any comment from the medical personnel.

''We've got something.'' The voice was masculine.

A jeans-clad woman in front of Tracy translated for the crowd. ''He has a heartbeat,'' she relayed.

A collective sigh of relief ran through the crowd. Without urging, they now responded to the request of the security guards to move back from the patient. Tracy slipped farther away, until a wall blocked her retreat.

It seemed only moments later that the paramedics transferred the stricken guest to a gurney and pushed him through the crowd to the waiting ambulance. The officers turned to talk to the teenagers.

Tracy looked toward the ashen woman in the lounge chair. Holding a cup in her shaking fingers, she stared into it while Clay signaled to someone nearby. A well-dressed young woman with a hotel logo pin on her lapel moved to Clay's side. Moments later, Clay took the cup from the shaking fingers and escorted the lady through the lobby to a waiting car. With a word to the wife, he nodded to his employee to accompany the distraught woman.

Tracy forced her feet to move across the lobby. She had to find out what had happened. She had to apologize. She reached Clay as the assistant manager met him.

Clay glanced at her and turned to the manager. "Did you see what happened?"

"No, I came after the paramedics."

Clay scanned the crowd. Some of them had moved away, others stood watching the police officers who had appeared on the scene. One man took pictures. Another made notes in a small book. Clay frowned. "We *would* have a group of travel writers here also."

Tracy hadn't thought she could feel worse, but she did. Travel writers. No wonder Clay had seemed excited about the weekend. A few good words in national newspapers and magazines could increase his business.

"Clay, I'm really sorry. I only tried to advertise Aunt Charli's chocolates to increase her business. You said . . ." She didn't complete the sentence, recalling the admiration in Clay's eyes when she'd told him about the scheme. "I didn't know it would create a riot."

He looked at her, his lips tightening as if he was holding back a flood of words. Then he sighed, shook his head once, and turned to his assistant.

"Call the hotel attorney and fill him in on the incident. You can send him reports later. I'll see what I can learn from the officers. Excuse me.'' He gave Tracy a faint smile and moved away.

Tracy weaved through the throng and pushed her way into the chocolate shop. Despite the smile, she knew she needn't worry about Clay's interest any longer. The look he'd given her was sympathetic, maybe pitying. *Irresponsible, inept.* He hadn't said the words, but what else could he think? He hadn't suggested she take the next flight to Taos, but she could sense it on the tip of his tongue. She'd not only fouled up Aunt Charli's business, she'd damaged Clay's. Future bookings for conferences were in jeopardy. Never mind that her goal had been to help Aunt Charli.

It was after three when Tracy managed to look up from the candy counter. Despite Clay's sending help to pass out samples, the line of young people didn't seem to be dwindling.

''Perhaps if I find the distributors and stop the source, we can catch up,'' Tracy said.

Madge nodded wearily.

Tracy struggled through the store and onto the sidewalk, and found one of her recruits in front of the hotel. She retrieved his fliers. It took an hour to find another familiar face having a cola break. Clutching the handful of fliers as if they were tainted money, Tracy turned toward the beach. Two hours later, she decided she must have contacted the last teenager. Carrying the precariously balanced fliers, she plodded across the warm sand.

Clay knew he had to find her. She'd looked so confused and despondent when she'd left the lobby. He felt guilty. She'd told him she wasn't a businesswoman. So why hadn't he offered to go over her plans with her and see if everything was running smoothly? Why hadn't he left his business associates to have breakfast without him?

He saw her walking wearily, head bent, away from the beach. Behind her, the sun was a crimson balloon sharing its magnificent color with the sky and the sea as it drifted slowly downward.

His heart swelling, he strode across the sand.

"Can I help you?"

She turned her head to gaze at him with somber eyes. "Help me dig a hole so I can crawl into it?" she said without spirit.

Clay reached for the slipping attack of fliers, shifted them to one arm, and slid his other hand beneath her elbow. "Let me help you back to firmer ground."

"Do you think that's possible?" Her voice was still lifeless.

"Ole Grandpa Winter used to tell me most things are possible with persistence."

"Persistence hasn't been high on my list of priorities lately."

Clay wanted to stop and take her in his arms and kiss her and tell her everything was all right, but he only tightened his grip on her elbow and helped her onto the walk. "See," he said cheerfully, "firmer ground."

"For now. Meanwhile, back at the ranch . . ." The tears that Clay hadn't wanted to see welled in Tracy's eyes.

"Are your guests crashing the lobby to cancel their reservations?"

"No," Clay said in an unusual drawl. "I believe

they may be dressing for a wine-tasting party in the Hibiscus Room, compliments of the hotel.''

He was pleased at the surprised look in Tracy's tearful eyes.

''You always think on the run and come out smelling of success.'' Her laughter was broken, but it wasn't a sob, Clay noted.

''Maybe not this time. I understand the kitchen staff is fearful of running out of cheese.''

''Oh?'' Tracy blinked her wet lashes.

''I told them to send out for pizza.''

''You didn't!'' Tracy's laughter improved.

''Well,'' he stalled, humor building in his own voice, ''I told them I had every confidence in their ability to cube the cheese smaller and fill in with fruit trays and hors d'oeuvres.''

''You really think a wine-tasting party will prevent your guests from departing, not to mention the bad publicity you'll get from the near riot in front of the hotel?'' Tracy turned serious again.

''I do.'' They walked past the hotel parking lot and along the now deserted walkway to the hotel. Clay pointed toward an unoccupied bench ahead of them. ''Can we stop and leave the sand in my shoes on the beach?''

Tracy sank down on the slatted bench and looked toward the ocean. ''Is that what's keeping my weary toes awake?''

Clay laughed and reached for her sandals. ''Seems I'm always taking your shoes off,'' he teased. He held her ankle in one hand and removed one sandal, shaking the contents back onto the sandy soil. Placing it on the bench, he reached for the other foot.

"What about the shop?" He had to think of something besides the sensation rippling through him when his fingers encountered the satiny texture of her ankle.

"The samples were gone before I left. I told Madge to give away candy as long as anyone came." She sighed. "We wouldn't have had any chocolates if one of your guests had come in—which is unlikely now, when they learn what caused the commotion."

"I don't know," Clay said lightly. "If I were you, I think I'd put on a night shift to refill the candy case. Tomorrow may be a bonus day after the local newspaper comes out."

Tracy reached for the sandal in Clay's hand. "I can put it on." She tugged her skirt over her legs and lifted one foot to prop it on her knee. Deftly, she threaded the sandal strap through the buckle.

Clay looked at her delicate wrists and tapered fingers with an increased awareness. His eyes skimmed the slender ankles visible beneath the concealing skirt. Again, he thought she was an enigma. Almost shy as she slid her long skirt down to cover her shapely legs; at other times exhibiting every curve in tight-fitting jeans and skin-hugging, flamboyant T-shirts.

His gaze went back to her face as she tilted her head and a spark from the lowering sun caught a silver earring and turned it to diamond..No, he reflected. Silver and turquoise became her more than diamonds.

Not that she wasn't classy. He'd seen her dressed in a fashionable suit, in chocolate-stained jeans, and last night in a frothy dress fit for a dream. He loved her in all of them.

He pulled his eyes away to tug off his right shoe.

Tracy reached a hand to his left arm as his right hand tipped the shoe over to dump the contents.

"What about the newspaper?" she asked. Trepidation tinged her voice again.

Clay shook the shoe efficiently before he answered her. Then he turned his charming smile in her direction.

"The boys from the beach . . ." He looked into her eyes, seeing the distress build up again. A breeze swept half a dozen strands of hair across her face, and he reached to gently brush them back.

"They weren't the cause of the disturbance." He spoke rapidly. He wanted to see the distress fade from those lovely eyes. He wanted to tell her he wasn't all work and no play and that he wanted to play with her. He'd change his life-style for her. He would.

"They were the solution," he said instead. "One of the conventioneers was unsteady when he got out of his car, and a teenager offered to help him to the lobby. When he fell, the young man yelled for his friend, and when the wife said her husband had a history of heart problems, the young men started CPR. Seems they'd just taken a course."

"The police . . ." Lines of consternation still formed between Tracy's eyes.

"The police were praising the young men, not pressuring them. The man has stabilized in intensive care. The paramedics said only good things about the procedures, the wife is ecstatic, and the local paper plans to make heroes of the boys. All that publicity can't do the hotel any harm. The pushing and shoving on the sidewalk won't even be noticed in the wake of the media report."

"But it could have been a disaster," Tracy replied in a quiet tone that said she wasn't convinced the roof still wouldn't fall in. "If I'd been more responsible . . ."

Clay touched her cheek, sliding his fingers down in a gentle caress to lift her chin and look into her eyes. "You did fine. You can't do everything and you delegated part of the work. You'll do better with practice."

"I don't want to do better in business, Clay. I don't want to be like my father, working sixteen hours a day to be a success. Mother says he claimed he was working to give us all the good things in life, but when she left, why did he keep working? He could have spent some time with me."

"Why is it you don't blame your mother for some of your lonely childhood?" Clay asked gently.

Tracy blinked her eyes slowly. "Despite my father's absence, I think I felt closer to him than to my mother. When Mother remarried, she said I'd be better off staying in a stable environment than traveling when her husband moved from job to job. I agreed. I still thought a house meant a home. I know better now. When I marry, I want more than a Sunday afternoon father for my children."

"I like that idea."

Distress clouded her eyes. "Clay." Her voice caught and deepened. "We're so different. We'd never be happy together."

"I'd be happy with you." His gaze mesmerized her.

"Until my unhappiness rubbed off on you."

"Do you like sailing?" Clay asked abruptly.

Tracy nodded slowly.

"We have something in common. Let's go sailing tomorrow and see if we can add to the list."

"Tomorrow? After today's fiasco?"

"Maybe tomorrow isn't a good day. Monday." He paused. "I have . . . Friday, for sure. I'll even leave the beeper in the car."

"I don't know," Tracy said.

Clay leaned forward and touched her lips with his. "Tracy, give us a chance. We could be the hottest item since Romeo and Juliet."

Laughter bubbled in Tracy's throat. "If that's the latest romance you've read, I think it's reasonably safe to spend a few hours on a sailboat with you."

"Don't be too sure. I watch movies."

"With your schedule, it's the late, late show, no doubt."

"What else!"

"Doris Day or Debbie Reynolds?"

"You'd rather I watched Sharon Stone?" Clay lifted an eyebrow and grinned devilishly.

Tracy giggled. "What time is this test run to take place?"

"I'll pick you up at eleven o'clock. We'll have lunch at the marina."

"The beeper will be in the car and the maître d' won't know your name?" Tracy made it a question.

"Absolutely."

"I'll meet you at the shop with my sneakers on."

"That wasn't so hard, was it? Just wait until I unfold the rest of my plans."

Clay stood up and pulled her to her feet. His right hand slid behind her head, the fingers entangling in her silken hair, and tipped her head back until her eyes met his. Farther along the walkway a light flickered on, its glow enhancing the color of her eyes. Clay heard the distant surf pounding in his ears and felt it dashing against the blood vessels in his neck. The light splashing across her face caressed the soft skin, giving it an ivory sheen that made her even lovelier. Her lips parted, and the indecision in her eyes faded. He lowered his mouth to hers.

She wasn't prepared for the sudden warmth as his lips touched hers. When she felt her knees would no longer hold her, he released her mouth. With one last, soft kiss, he released his hold on her and turned to pick up the leaflets he'd placed on the bench. Without breaking the silence, he cupped Tracy's elbow and guided her toward the hotel entrance.

Still feeling shaken when he released her arm, Tracy bade him good-bye and watched him stride toward the hotel. The shaky feeling was replaced by a vague sense of loss, even with his kiss still warm on her lips.

Of course, he had to check with his hotel personnel about the party or any aftermath rumbles from the afternoon's disturbance. Just as she had to check in at the shop. He hadn't promised to change overnight.

Besides, one afternoon with Clay wasn't a commitment for life, was it?

She frowned. Why had she added a question to the end of a statement?

Chapter Eight

Tracy rolled the wheelchair from the hotel beauty salon, where she'd left Aunt Charli earlier, trying to scan the lobby unobtrusively while maneuvering through the room. Clay had better things to do on Tuesdays than stand around greeting incoming guests, but just knowing he was somewhere in the hotel brought a pleasurable feeling.

"Were you able to get all the supplies while I was in the beauty shop?" Aunt Charli queried.

Tracy turned the chair toward the hall leading to the shops. "Not everything. Maybe I'll drive to L.A. tomorrow."

Slowing the chair, she parked it at the inside entrance of the shop and went around to prop the door open. Returning, she weighted the rear of the wheelchair with her right foot, raising the small front wheels over the door sill, and carefully shoved the chair forward until the larger back wheels rolled inside.

Aunt Charli peered at the candy case and turned her head to slant a look at Tracy. "I called Consuelo, a former part-timer, to come in for a few days. You mentioned the candy supply is low."

"I'm sure we can use the help." Tracy glanced behind the untended counter. Madge or Sonjia usually appeared at the sound of the door opening. She pushed the door closed and grasped the chair handles again, weaving past the small circular table to guide the chair around the end of the counter. She paused to eye the slightly lowered door sill to the kitchen. The physical therapist who'd instructed Aunt Charli in the use of the chair had said something about backing into elevators. She frowned in concentration. But had he said to pull the chair backwards when a doorway dropped a couple of inches? It made sense to her. She renewed her grip on the handles and attempted to swing the chair around in the confined space. A front wheel balked.

"Sorry," she said in a singsong to Aunt Charli. "I should have taken a wheelchair course."

"I'm sure you can do it," Aunt Charli said. The tenseness in her voice was barely discernible.

Tracy took a deep breath, eyed the suddenly narrowing doorway warily, and pulled the chair toward her. She cut the wheels and backed toward the opening. The overlarge wheel jarred against the wall. With difficulty, she avoided expelling her breath in a rush of frustration.

"Do you know what this reminds me of, Aunt Charli?" she said wryly. She didn't wait for an answer. "Remember my clumsy efforts to back into a parking space when you tried to teach me to drive?"

"You weren't clumsy," Charli objected.

"You were eager for me to enroll in a driver's ed class." Tracy pushed the chair forward and managed to turn the wheels.

"Not because you were clumsy. I wasn't a good teacher. How you learned to drive with me as a teacher is still a mystery."

"The same way I learned to make candy." Tracy scraped the wheel of the chair against the casing trim of the opening, and her gaze jerked to the wheel where Charli's hand rested. Charli was already withdrawing the fingers looped over the side of the rubber.

Tracy expelled her indrawn breath slowly and pulled the chair back an inch to reposition the wheels. "You nagged me until I got it right."

She was rewarded with a laugh from her aunt. "If I remember, my nagging concerned your 'tasting' eating into my profit."

This time Tracy laughed. The wheels rolled over the sill with a slight bump, the aroma of chocolate increased, and she looked down lovingly at her aunt's newly colored strawberry locks. Her father had spent most of his time with clients, her mother, after leaving Costa Corona, had moved from one country to another, but she'd always known where to find Charli. Charli hadn't been the parental type, but just knowing she was at the shop had been a kind of security. But it wasn't enough for a child if there could be more, Tracy reminded herself. She pushed the thought away and lifted her gaze to peer around the quiet room.

The huge copper kettle, the shining microwave ovens, and the polished marble counter were as untended as the front of the shop. A bowl of melted chocolate accounted for the fresh aroma.

Tracy glanced toward the hallway leading to the rest room in puzzlement, wondering if Madge was in the rest room. Or was it Sonjia? Maybe one of them was late coming in. Charli's fidgeting brought her attention back to the chair as the uninjured foot slipped off the metal footrest in search of the floor.

"Help me onto a stool and you can push this unwieldy thing in the back hall. That is, if it'll fit." Charli wiggled her body to the edge of the chair.

The chair moved, Tracy gripped the handles firmly, and the missing candymakers slipped from her thoughts.

"Don't move until the brakes are on." Anxiety made her voice sharper than she intended. "Give me time," she added lamely. "I'll get to know my way around this chair."

She bent to reach to the side of one wheel, pressing a lever forward until a clicking sound indicated the brake was secure, then she reached for the opposite lever. Satisfied that the wheels were locked in place, she walked to the front of the chair to assist her aunt to her feet. She stopped and turned around at a sound from beyond the tiny hallway. Even as she wondered about the sound, it came again, a muted coughing intermingled with a coarser sound. Tracy's shoulders slumped. Apparently whoever was here should have called in sick!

Going around the table, she pushed the melted chocolate and empty seashell molds toward Charli. Madge hadn't appeared by the time she'd supplied Charli with tea towels and utensils.

Finally, she went to the hallway and called toward the closed door at the end. The door opened narrowly and Madge answered in a weak voice. A moment later, she opened the door wider and leaned against the frame. Pale-faced, she grinned weakly at Tracy. "I guess I didn't really get over the flu. Or I have a relapse or something."

Tracy thought of the depleted stock of chocolates and swallowed the panic before it could arise. She nodded sympathetically. "Sounds like you need to be home in bed." She brightened her voice. "Aunt Charli called Consuelo. She should be here at ten. With Aunt Charli and Sonjia and Lindon, we're overstaffed."

"Overstaffed?" Madge croaked. "Sonjia is going to be late and none of them are here at the same time."

"Connie is staying all day."

Madge closed her eyes briefly. "I'd argue, but I'd be more hindrance than help—and you're gonna need help today."

"I'm sure you and Aunt Charli have had empty candy cases before."

"But we didn't have orders for a bridge party on Wednesday, two, or is it three, luncheons in the hotel this week, and a wedding reception on the weekend. Not to forget those white chocolate baskets you promised Mrs. Washburn." Madge's eyelids fluttered weakly. "Oh, yes. You'll find a number to call back, a caterer who's anxious to talk to you. A friend of Mr. Winter's, who's apparently touting our wares."

Tracy nodded. Even when she managed to forget

Clay for a moment, someone was always around to remind her.

Charli grinned broadly. "I don't know about Tracy, since it increases her workload, but I appreciate any help in the advertising department."

Charli was still grinning, though somewhat wearily, at six when Tracy drove her home.

Settling Charli comfortably in front of the television set, with a bag of fast food and her crutches nearby, Tracy hesitated.

"You don't mind if I go back to the shop and work on the baskets, do you? It takes me longer than you to make one."

"I'll be fine." Charli repositioned her injured leg atop the ottoman. "Don't work too late. The candy will be there tomorrow."

Tracy drove back through the fast-food lane, picked up a super-size cola and returned to the shop. During the drive, the chocolate-latticed baskets didn't enter her mind once. But the brown-eyed CEO of Winter's Inn never left it. She'd been in the kitchen most of the day and hadn't seen Clay entering or leaving the hotel. If he came for his occasional truffle, she'd missed him. She sighed. Friday seemed so far away.

Bidding Lindon good night, she started closing the door slowly while her gaze wandered to the hotel entrance. Her heart thudded eagerly. Clay strode along the walkway leading to the shop, his gaze meeting hers.

"I was afraid I'd miss you." He breathed easily, his gaze running over her face warmly. "Just closing up?"

"I'm going to work in the kitchen a little while."

She held the door open, inviting him to enter. "Come and watch. I'll ply you with sweets."

"Wish I could." He pulled his mouth into a humorous frown. "But I'm on my way to a meeting."

Tracy's thudding heart slowed. But the cryptic remark about his work didn't surface. After all, wasn't she still in the shop?

"The meeting should be over about ten. Could I interest you in a cup of cappuccino about that time?"

Her heart resumed its excited beat. "I'll be here."

Clay moved nearer and tilted his head to cover her lips with a brief kiss. "So will I." He released her hand reluctantly and walked toward the path to the parking lot.

Collecting bowls and bags of white, lavender, and sky blue chocolate, Tracy placed them on the counter. Then she propped the open instruction book on the table and added pans and packages of lollipop sticks to her work space.

While her fingers rolled the warm candy into long cords and wove them between the candy-coated sticks, thoughts of Clay wove warmly through her mind. When she wasn't thinking about Clay, her mind pondered what to wear on Friday. She concocted long, humorous conversations with Clay, tossed her short hair in an imaginary breeze, and caught herself laughing out loud as the sound reverberated in the quiet kitchen.

Clay returned while she was still working.
"I could help so you'll get through faster.
Tracy grinned.

"All right." He returned the grin. "I meant wash up."

He removed the charcoal coat of his suit, and looked around for a coatrack. "In the hall," Tracy gestured. "But really, Clay, you needn't."

"I want to." He collected empty bowls and carried them to the sink. Returning, he picked up the spoons, raising one to his mouth to lick the contents.

Tracy couldn't stop smiling.

He rinsed the bowls and stacked them in the dishwasher. Closing the door, he turned to Tracy with a grin. "I was a busboy in the hotel kitchen one summer. Maybe I should keep in practice in case this current job falls through."

He raised an arm and used the back of his hand to push the wayward hair from his forehead. Chocolate-smeared knuckles painted a wave resembling a three-year-old's finger-painting practice across his forehead.

Involuntarily, Tracy giggled.

"You wouldn't hire me?" he queried humorously.

She rolled her eyes. "I don't think your forte is dishwashing any more than it is candymaking."

"Did I do so badly with candymaking?"

"Let's say Aunt Charli couldn't afford you. As she said to me earlier, my tasting habits as a teenager ate into her profits."

"I don't remember tasting that much."

"It wasn't the tasting, it was the dripping," Tracy teased. Her eyes met his and she thought it would be worth losing a few pounds of chocolate just to have him in the kitchen.

He walked to the counter to retrieve a spoon and dipped his head to place a kiss on Tracy's lips. Carrying the spoon to the faucet, he rinsed it and then turned to give her an enchanting smile. ''I'm rinsing dishes, not dripping chocolate. I can't think of any financial burden in that.''

Tracy gestured at the swash of chocolate smeared by the spoon as he'd leaned to kiss her. ''Not if you don't count laundry bills.'' Giggling, she handed him a tea towel. ''There's a mirror in the hallway.''

He eyed the chocolate stain on his shirt. ''My jacket will cover it.''

''I mean for your face.'' She pushed him toward the hallway and followed to point to the mirror on the wall.

Watching him look at the chocolate-painted image with a trace of embarrassment followed by a humorous scowl, she felt a rush of tenderness. The usually well-groomed man whose smile could charm the teeth out of a business tycoon could also smile at himself. Winking at her in the mirror, he raised the cloth to his forehead and scrubbed at the skin like a mischievous schoolboy.

Turning to present his face for inspection, he pulled down the corners of his mouth. ''Am I presentable enough to escort you to the café?''

Tracy nodded with mock seriousness. She'd have gone with him if his face was completely covered in chocolate, but she couldn't tell him that. In fact, she couldn't tell herself that. He hadn't changed. Just as Friday's date couldn't change anything. He was still a workaholic and she still held on to her dreams. But the date could be added to her dreams.

* * *

As could the late evening cappuccino on the patio overlooking the ocean, Tracy mused dreamily after she had returned to Charli's guest room. She pulled on a long T-shirt and slipped into bed.

She was in love with him, but a long-term relationship wouldn't work. She would worry about his health, simmer silently when he didn't spend time with her, and turn into a nagging witch. Which would give him reason to spend more time at work. Hadn't she seen it happen?

She pushed the morose thoughts away and concentrated on the sailing trip. If memories were the only treasure she would carry with her back to Taos, she would make them as wonderful as possible. She wanted to be with him for the day. She wanted him to kiss her, she wanted to feel the shiver of excitement when his hands caressed her skin. She wanted a memory, a Technicolor memory with sound. She wanted to remember the smell of the sea and the sight of the breeze ruffling his sun-gilded hair. She wanted to remember his dark brown pupils flecked with light and laughter. She wanted a mental picture of the white caps ruffling the ocean as the seagulls glided gracefully overhead to the sound of a soft, lilting melody from a radio. He might not be the one who'd sit beside her the rest of the evenings of her life, but he'd be the one in her heart forever.

Having agreed to meet Clay at the shop, since she had to drive Charli there, Tracy pushed the wheelchair along the sidewalk and marveled at the glorious weather. Clouds like airy islands of white meringue floated over the sun-touched sea. A beautiful day for sailing. She'd dressed casually, as Clay had suggested, pulling on well-worn jeans and a T-shirt and borrowing a cobalt blue pullover from Aunt Charli.

She couldn't suppress her eagerness. She told herself it was because the sky was unusually blue, the clouds were incredibly white, and the smell of the sea was like rare perfume. But she knew it was the thought of being with Clay that filled her with euphoria.

It was wrong to let her emotions overpower her common sense, but it was just for today.

She left Aunt Charli with Madge, in the kitchen. She endured a few teasing remarks and hurried back to the front of the store.

Her heart leaped at the sight of Clay. He looked devastatingly handsome dressed in white duck trousers and a dark blue pullover. The briefcase he carried looked out of place.

"We have a problem."

Despair, like a deluge of dark water, washed through Tracy, threatening to send her heart in a downward spiral. She glanced at the briefcase. She should have known!

"Or, rather, the sailboat has a problem," Clay continued with a grin. "But we're still going sailing—sort of sailing."

"What's 'sort of sailing'?" Hope rose warily.

"Sailing in the air. Flying."

Sailing, swimming, flying. Did it make a difference as long as she was with Clay? "If you mean sailing off the cliffs on one of those hang gliders, count me out." Her humorous tone belied her words. "I like to fly in big planes with more than one engine."

"I was thinking of a Cessna 172. It will take us to Catalina for lunch better than a 747."

Tracy's heart floated upward like a helium-filled balloon. She didn't care how they went to Santa Catalina. The way she felt, she could fly there without the aid of a plane. Her feet barely touched ground on the walk to the car, and she was still soaring when they reached the airport.

Parking the car, Clay slid from the driver's seat and reached for the briefcase. "You can wait here while I see if the plane is ready. I won't be long." He turned to stride across the asphalt to a nearby building. Tracy's gaze followed his figure, her gaze lingering on the broad shoulders and lean hips. Almost as an afterthought, the gaze turned humorously on the briefcase. Did it hold a master key to the hotel safe or the wine cellar? Then a suspicious thought crept into mind. A mobile telephone? Semantics! He'd promised to leave his beeper in the car, but he hadn't mentioned a telephone.

In the distance, she saw him returning and struggled to regain her composure. She hadn't intended for this day to lead to more than a pleasant outing. So why was she upset to find he had a line open to his work as usual? She would ignore the briefcase and concentrate on having a good time. She hadn't been to the island for years.

But her mind still railed at Clay's apparent duplicity. She clenched her hands, feeling the nails of her fingers piercing her palms as her emotions seesawed between anger and distress. With an effort, she quelled the rising anger, got a grip on the distress, and displayed a smile as Clay approached to open the door for her.

"We're ready to go."

Tracy followed him, eyeing the row of small planes with less enthusiasm than she'd felt earlier. He approached the third plane in line, its long body as sleek and graceful as a dolphin with wings; the satiny coating white as summer clouds on a clear day. He extended a hand to help her in.

The cabin held four seats, and he motioned for her to sit in the front passenger seat. A moment later, he slid into the one next to it. Tracy looked at him quizzically. "Where's the pilot?"

"You're looking at him." He handed her the briefcase. "Hold this a minute."

She eyed the case and couldn't restrain her comment. "I thought this was a play day. Is the briefcase really necessary?"

"Absolutely. Wouldn't fly without it. I might need a map, or instructions. . . ."

Tracy's heart leaped. It wasn't an umbilical cord back to the hotel switchboard. "You need to take the instruction book," Tracy said in mock distress. Her voice felt as bubbly as her heart. "Do you really know how to fly?"

"The instructor at the flight school was satisfied."

"Did this instruction include hands-on experience?"

"Some." Clay's eyes scanned the instrument panel, pausing briefly at intervals.

"Uum." Tracy watched his hands deftly open the throttle slightly and turn on the master switch. He seemed to follow a mental checklist as he engaged the

starter and advanced the throttle. Only when he
seemed to have the throttle at the setting he wanted
did he turn his attention to Tracy with a raised eyebrow.

"Ready?"

"Is it too late to ask how long you've been flying?"
Not that she cared, her heart sang. The buoyancy soaring through her could keep them airborne to Hawaii.

"Two hundred hours or so."

"Hours," Tracy yelped, watching Clay's gaze return to the panel in front of him. "I'm talking years."

"Hours are years in flying. Now relax. You're safer
in the sky than on the freeway." Clay scanned the
runway and Tracy's gaze followed his. An executive
jet landed with a controlled scream and taxied to the
parking area, its turbine winding down so a normal
level of airport noise resumed.

Clay taxied off the apron and Tracy closed her eyes
momentarily. She felt the rise when the plane left the
ground, and she heard Clay's soft laughter.

"If you don't open your eyes soon, we'll be landing
and you'll have missed a beautiful view."

"Landing? How long does it take to get to Catalina?" She opened her eyes to narrow slits, glancing
swiftly at the receding landscape.

"Ah, twenty miles," Clay mused. "One hundred
and twenty miles an hour . . . Maybe ten to fifteen
minutes—to the airport. A bit longer to get to Avalon
for lunch. The field is six or seven hundred feet above
the city and we have to take a bus down the mountain."

Tracy widened her eyes, released the breath she

hadn't realized she'd imprisoned, and watched with interest as Clay punched numbers on a little black box.

He smiled at her inquisitive look. "This is a controlled area. I'm checking in with Departure Control, who'll track the plane."

Tracy nodded as if that explained the whole puzzling procedure and turned to peer past the wing below her. The sea was a dazzling blue-green coverlet supporting a recreational flotilla of sailboats, motorboats, and cabin cruisers on the glittering, sequined surface. In the distance, a magnificent ocean liner chugged toward the harbor of Long Beach.

"That's Avalon in the distance." Clay claimed her attention. "I'll fly over it so you can see the harbor and city from the air."

Tracy leaned toward her window. She'd traveled to Santa Catalina Island, with Jolie when she was sixteen, on the day cruise ship that sailed from Long Beach, and again with her fiancé when she was in college. She'd never seen it from the air.

The twenty-two-mile-long island with its rise of chaparral-studded mountains loomed in front of them, and then they were over the bay with a colorful array of seagoing craft bobbing gently on the blue water below the plane. The bright roof of the Catalina Casino filled Tracy's sight, and then she recognized a sprawling mansion, once the summer home of the chewing gum magnate William Wrigley, Jr., and now an elegant inn. Then Clay turned the aircraft toward the airport high above the cove.

He circled the field and turned to land the plane on the asphalt, on what looked like the top of a mountain.

Taxiing to the side of the runway, Clay parked the

plane, tying it down while Tracy watched. When they walked to the nearby buildings, Tracy noticed he'd left his briefcase in the plane. She was momentarily embarrassed. She'd been wrong about the cellular phone. When she thought about it, she'd been wrong about other things too. Clay's only care wasn't about business. He cared about his father, he cared about his employees, he cared about his tenants. A few weeks ago she would have said it all came under the heading of business, she mused. Now, she called it commendable. It was difficult to hang on to that long-ago resentment with the sun warming her skin and Clay's gaze warming her inside.

Clay motioned toward the building as he walked to her side. "This way." He fell in step with her. "I think this is the only landing field where I've ever had to pay landing fees. That's because it's privately owned."

Tracy nodded as if she understood why being privately owned made it different and accompanied Clay inside. She gazed around the small room, catching snatches of the conversation between Clay and a young woman.

"Enjoy your stay on the island," the young woman added, after she'd collected the landing fee. Clay started to turn but her voice stopped him.

"Oh, Mr. Winter. I have a message for you to call the hotel as soon as you arrive."

Tracy gritted her teeth. Clay didn't need a cellular phone or a beeper. If he was on a deserted island, the hotel manager would send smoke signals.

Clay glanced at Tracy and smiled. "I promised you

an uninterrupted lunch.'' He thanked the woman and asked about transportation to Avalon.

''The bus should be here soon,'' she told them and turned back to the papers on the counter.

The small bus took them on a curving, clattering ride downhill on a narrow road that weaved through lush foliage and prickly chaparral. Tracy gripped the edge of the seat, her gaze darting between the curving road and the driver who used a handheld radio to keep in touch with someone. The bus swerved unexpectedly, stopping in a pull-out area, and moments later another bus careened past with a whoosh of wheels and rumble of engine.

Tracy found her breath and felt Clay's touch on her arm. She turned her head and followed his motioning hand. ''Wild mountain goat,'' he said. But Tracy turned around too late to see it.

''A herd of buffalo also inhabit the island, along with the goats and wild boar. Dad brought me along on a hunting trip once. Wild boar, I think. Not that he hunted. He only wanted to get away, as he phrased it.''

When the bus parked, Tracy stepped off with Clay and viewed the small picturesque city with delight. The disturbing telephone call was barely a whisper in her memory. The balmy breeze ruffling the palm fronds brought a sense of romance to the holiday atmosphere.

They strolled the sloping streets, browsing in quaint shops. They stopped to watch a colony of sea lions basking in the sun. They talked about the time each had been to hear a band in the ballroom of the casino.

Then Clay guided her to a charming restaurant with an equally charming view.

But lunch was not quite as enjoyable as Tracy had envisioned. The waiter was attentive, the food was tasty, and lovely music played in the background; The view of blue water and bobbing white boats was a photographer's fantasy. The red-roofed Catalina Casino, with its Moroccan-inspired architecture, promised hours of entertainment inside its walls. On the beach, toddlers built castles on the sand and sunbathing couples built castles in the air, and beyond the vase of pink and white carnations centered on the blue tablecloth, Clay fidgeted.

She glanced at him while they pondered over the dessert tray, sparring teasingly over a choice of carrot cake—her favorite—and a delectable raspberry-chocolate creation their server touted.

Sampling the restaurant's new creation, Clay stopped fidgeting briefly, but Tracy could see the unrest in his eyes. While he waited for the waiter to return with his credit card and bill, Tracy took a deep, calming breath.

"I'll finish my coffee if you want to call the hotel before we go on the bicycle tour."

Sipping coffee after he left, she found it was her turn to fidget. But what else could she have said? He would have looked miserable until he knew why he'd been called, and she'd have felt miserable knowing he'd rather be at the hotel. Still, she'd play it cool. Even if he told her they must return on the next jitney to the airport.

Clay's approach was casual, his eyes revealing nothing. He signed the luncheon check, pocketed his credit card, and smiled at Tracy. "Ready to go?" His smile looked like it had run out of energy.

"Is the hotel still standing?" Tracy asked, striving for humor.

"Not quite that bad. It's flooding."

A flash of Aunt Charli rolling her wheelchair through a pool of water made her look at Clay in consternation. "How can it be flooding? We haven't had rain for weeks."

"Broken sewer pipe. It's leaking into the kitchen. The water supply is threatened with contamination."

Tracy looked at him silently.

"My assistant must decide whether to close the hotel to incoming guests and cancel receptions and dinner parties if there is a danger of food, ice, and water being contaminated. It's not a decision he wants to make alone."

Tracy nodded soberly. It wasn't as if Clay had planned to be called.

"I told him I'd keep in touch." He caught her hand in his. "Now, what about getting on with my plan to show you the city over the handlebars of a bicycle." His jovial tone echoed none of his concern over the hotel problem.

Renting bicycles, they toured the paths suggested by the shop owner. Laughter erupted between them frequently, but not often enough to suppress Tracy's concern at the troubled line creasing Clay's forehead during unguarded moments. Relief overcame disappointment when he suggested they return to the mainland.

Chapter Nine

" "I'm sorry, Tracy."

Clay repeated his apology five minutes after they'd taken off from the island airport.

"I know." Tracy gazed solemnly over the right wing of the Cessna at the shimmering sea strewn with pleasure boats.

"Next week," Clay promised, "I'll make it up to you. We'll take the sailboat, start early, and spend the day in Santa Catalina."

"You sound just like my father." Tracy was appalled that she'd said the words. But they were out, and they were true.

"Maybe the same words, Tracy. But I mean them," Clay said soberly. "I'm sorry about the sewer pipe leakage. It could be threatening the health of my hotel guests."

Tracy felt like she had no control over her voice.

"If it wasn't a water pipe, it would be something else." She hated the thoughts she'd expressed, hated the note of dreariness she heard in her voice. She should be thanking Clay for an exciting trip and a lovely lunch, but she sounded like a spoiled child disappointed over a lost·pony ride.

"That's hotel business," Clay said. His voice strove for humor.

Tracy averted her face, shielding the scowl she felt must be evident from Clay. She stared dully at the sea below, following half a dozen small motorboats skimming toward the island. Was this how it had been with her parents? Even when they were together, they were arguing over being apart. The boats moved farther away, looking like little more than colored corks bobbing in the water, and she forced the dullness from her eyes and the scowl from her face. She was a twenty-six-year-old woman who'd learned, or thought she'd learned, to deal with disappointment long ago. That's all this was—a disappointing trip—a disappointing date. Wasn't it?

How could she fault Clay for her disappointment? The trip had been wonderful. He'd treated her to everything he'd promised. So why couldn't she concentrate on his good intentions instead of the call from the hotel—the call back to business, the familiar words that echoed broken promises from her childhood?

The coast appeared through the windscreen, and moments later the plane passed over the waves rolling toward the shore to spread a skirt of lace-edged water on the sand and tease the toes of daring toddlers. Tracy dismissed her thoughts, resolving to be a better companion.

She was relieved that landing, parking, and changing from an open skyway to a crowded freeway limited conversation. By the time Clay walked her to the chocolate shop, she had found her manners. She thanked him graciously, managing a smile that was almost gay.

Clay returned the smile. "My pleasure," he replied. The look in his eyes reinforced his words, and yet Tracy sensed an urgency in his stance, like a racer listening for the starting gun. "I'll call you as soon as things settle down. Maybe we can have dinner tonight."

Tracy hesitated. "I don't think so, Clay. I . . . I need some time."

A puzzled look clouded Clay's eyes. His lips parted, then closed, and he looked toward the hotel.

"I'll call you," he repeated. He turned to leave and paused. "Let me know if the sewer leak threatens Charli's kitchen."

A new shock of distress ran through Tracy. She'd been so absorbed in her own misery she hadn't thought about Charli's kitchen. She blinked and nodded at Clay. "Of course."

For a moment, she was startled. Worrying about Charli even while he thought the hotel might be in danger was so like Clay. In the past few weeks, she'd come to realize he cared about his tenants and his guests and his employees. So what if that concern came under the normal course of business?

She watched him stride toward the lobby, and a sense of loss swept through her. The pain that had only started when she'd looked into Clay's puzzled eyes at her rebuff now increased. She waited until he passed through the glass doorway and then she turned toward the shop and took a deep breath. Why couldn't Clay be the man she wanted him to be instead of the workaholic he was?

"I hear the hotel has a problem." Charli lifted her head to look at Tracy, continuing to dip caramel blocks into melted chocolate. "Figured you and Clay would be back sooner than you planned."

So what else is new? Tracy kept the thought to herself and stuffed her purse on a shelf. "Any problem with flooding at the shop?"

"No. The hotel kitchen is lower than the shop. I don't think we'll have a problem."

"Clay said to call if you did." Tracy tied an apron over her jeans and trudged to the sink to wash her hands.

"Don't start to work. I'll just finish up this batch and we can go home."

"You're sure?" Tracy dried her hands. She didn't want to stay at the shop. Still, she didn't want to go home. Watching television wouldn't banish thoughts of Clay. Waiting for Charli to coat the last caramel, Tracy carried the finished tray of candy to a cooling shelf. Charli was struggling to push the wheelchair up the small rise to the front room when she returned. She pushed the chair over the rise and returned to get her purse. Thanking Consuelo for cleaning up, she waved and followed the wheelchair.

Charli wheeled the chair deftly around the candy counter, passed by the circular table displaying her June theme bridal basket laden with a floral bouquet of chocolates, and almost screeched to a halt to wait for Tracy to open the door.

"Jolie called," she said. "She's at her parents' house and has tickets to the opera—the Saturday matinee at the Performing Arts Center. I don't remember the name—I have trouble telling one from the other. I never understand the story, but I love to go for the marvelous stage settings and costumes."

"I can't go to an opera. Tomorrow is Saturday."

"I've already asked Connie to come in." Charli waved impatiently at the door. "Which fast-food place tonight?"

Despite her repeated argument that she couldn't take Saturday afternoon off, Tracy felt relieved when Charli insisted. She didn't want to see Clay and, of course, he'd be at the hotel. So she didn't want to be at the shop. She was ready and anxiously waiting for Jolie by one o'clock.

"What are you doing in California again?"

"I may get transferred to Los Angeles," Jolie said with a show of exuberance. "Wouldn't it be nice if you transferred back to California too? You could drive to see me one weekend and I could drive to the beach the next."

"Would your boyfriend approve?"

"Well," Jolie drawled, "maybe we'd have to make it once a month. Unless we can double-date," she added, as if she'd just had the thought. "Me and my guy and you and the handsome CEO at the hotel . . ." She let the sentence dangle.

"Tell me about the transfer," Tracy said, giving her no time to pursue the thought.

They were walking to the theater surrounded by stately buildings before Jolie mentioned the subject again. ''What do you think? Double-dating, like old times?''

Tracy hated to lie to Jolie, and yet she couldn't bring herself to pour out her problems to her friend. ''Do you think we'd better find our seats? I hate to stumble over feet after the lights go down.''

Jolie nodded, looking at the tickets and motioning with her left hand.

Tracy opened her program, pretending to study it while scanning the surroundings. Beautifully dressed people walked in the aisles, some nodding to acquaintances and friends before they took their seats. Then the aisle traffic and murmuring and rustling stopped, and the house was silent as the lovely lights dimmed.

Tracy lowered her program and joined in the applause as the conductor appeared, threading his way expertly through the violins. The music sounded and the curtains floated back, and Tracy's eyes widened at the marvelous setting. Entranced, she gazed at the people on stage, each costume appearing to her more lavish and spectacular than the last. She thrilled to the arias, felt a rise of excitement listening to the opening chorus, and realized why Aunt Charli didn't need to follow the story to enjoy the opera.

Her mind wandered before the chorus finished. The stage blurred before her, and the music became a backdrop for her thoughts.

Yesterday had started so well. She mused over the flight, remembering Clay's attention to the details as he started the plane. She remembered the bright roof of the casino and the sea lions. She remembered the dessert they'd argued over and her eager capitulation because she thought Clay wanted to try the raspberry dessert. She tried to forget Clay's return to the table after the telephone call and couldn't. It would always be that way with Clay. She laughed silently and wryly. He'd probably answer the telephone if they were on their honeymoon.

The chorus stopped and Tracy focused on the stage. She could leave soon. Aunt Charli had her former workers at the shop and her part-time housekeeper at the condo. She'd known all along she was going back to Taos. A new voice on the stage lifted with a haunting, sad quality that permeated her thoughts, enhancing her own sorrow at the thought of never seeing Clay again. A pain sliced through her chest. It dulled to an ache as she forced her eyes to concentrate on the singer and the scene.

She would keep herself busy until it came time to leave. Too busy to think about Clay, she told herself as the house lights came on.

"Isn't it thrilling?" Jolie marveled. She shifted and stood up. "Shall we go downstairs for refreshments?"

Tracy nodded, followed her down the crowded aisle, and accompanied her to request a drink from a busy bartender.

Over ice-cold Perrier in long-stemmed glasses, Tracy observed the other people sipping their beverages. Some were dressed elaborately for an afternoon performance, others wore high heels and daytime dresses.

Jolie turned at the sound of her name and, a moment later, introduced Tracy to two young women dressed in long skirts. Then it was time for the next act and Jolie waved as they made their way back to their seats.

"Cory asked us to go to dinner with them. I said yes. You don't have to get back to the shop, do you?"

Tracy shook her head and looked at the stage, relieved that conversation was forestalled with the dimming of the lights. It was a good start to keeping busy, she mused.

She managed to concentrate on the program after that. The group met for drinks at a trendy bar and went to dinner, and later to a disco. Tracy only thought of Clay in bits and pieces. Bidding Jolie good night and entering the condo, Tracy thought she must be tired enough to sleep. But she was wrong. She was still checking the time at five o'clock. Then Charli was calling her for coffee and it was almost eleven and time to take Charli to the shop.

The water contamination problem hadn't reached the shop, but it had kept Clay at the hotel, Charli disclosed. "He called. Said he'd call again today."

Tracy didn't reply to the message. Instead, she filled in the silence with a report on the elegant costumes and the magnificent settings of the opera.

She managed to be too busy to answer the telephone when Clay called, and by Sunday evening, she suggested to Charli that they drive to San Diego for dinner.

"I know you must be tired of going from the shop to home and vice versa. A drive will be good for you."

"The wheelchair is so much trouble," Charli protested. "I see you struggling to get it in the trunk."

"It's not that hard," Tracy countered. She wheeled the cumbersome chair out the door and toward the parking lot, scanning the hotel entrance for a sign of Clay. She didn't want to see him, she told herself. She was looking for him to avoid running into him.

The coast highway was crowded with homeward-bound traffic, but the cars moved steadily. Maneuvering the car through the traffic kept Tracy from thinking of Clay. Almost.

"Have you asked Clay when he is expecting the next convention group?" Charli asked.

"Not really," Tracy said with a dry laugh.

She watched the traffic, threading through lanes to reach the freeway on-ramp.

Charli waited until the car moved onto the freeway before she spoke again. "Things will go better next time." She smoothed a strawberry tress back into her carefully coiffed hair. "Madge says we did get a number of hotel guests in. Last-minute gifts for those at home. I think we should try it again."

"I've been thinking about that," Tracy said. She was reluctant to say how much, because thinking of the hotel guests meant thinking of Clay, and she spent too much doing time doing that. Her new idea involved seeing Clay again to ask his permission because it concerned his employees and his guests. She didn't want to do it. But she should. Didn't Charli still need help?

"What did you come up with?"

"Leaving a Charli's coupon on the pillow with the seashell treat."

"If the guests stayed two weeks, they wouldn't need to buy a box of chocolates," Charli said wryly.

"I meant only on the day of arrival. The maids must know which rooms have new guests. Would it be much trouble to slip a coupon under the bedside treat?"

"I don't know. Have you discussed it with Clay?"

Tracy concentrated on passing a car. "Not yet. I thought I might send a letter so you would have an okay in writing if he approves."

"Oh, he will. Clay is anxious for the shop to stay in the hotel."

"I'd like more than an 'it sounds good to me' agreement. He wasn't pleased with the disturbance our first coupons caused. He's always thinking how things will affect the hotel. He'll probably have to discuss it with his manager or the head of housekeeping or his accountant. Then he'll wonder if letting you advertise your chocolates could mean he must let all the shop owners advertise in some way. Clay won't see it as a 'little coupon on the pillow.' "

"He might. You're pretty hard on Clay."

"Just because I'm beginning to think like him."

"I rather like that. With your energy and fresh ideas, Charli's Chocolates may not have to move to a sidewalk food truck. In fact, one of my old customers suggested we contact the better department stores with a sample of our wares."

"Your wares, Aunt Charli. I have to go back to my job in Taos sometime."

"Don't you think it's time you came home? Besides, I thought you and young Clay Winter were getting along well."

"Too well," Tracy grumbled under her breath.

Charli apparently heard her. "Something wrong with that?"

"Only that he's just like Dad. His main focus is making the hotel a success. He can't get away from it for a day. The manager even called him when we went to Catalina, and he had to fly right back to the hotel."

"Ooh." Charli shook her head slowly. "Delcy's voice is echoing in the background."

"Well, I can see how Mother felt now. Can you blame her for hating Dad's neglect? I can't remember him taking me anywhere after she left, and he was seldom home. I can imagine how Mother felt at the lack of attention. I've heard her say, often enough, that if Dad did take her somewhere she expected him to be called away—so they took two cars."

"You think if Clay's like your father and you are like your mother, a marriage would never work."

"Well," Tracy said defensively, "it wouldn't."

"As hard as you try to be carefree and footloose, you are not like your mother, Tracy. It wasn't only your father's working that caused her to leave him. They had nothing in common. Not even love, after a few years. I think she liked the idea of being married to a young attorney. She expected a busy social life. She'd been a reporter and she liked people and action. The social life, the traveling, the companionship with her present husband is what she wanted. I don't think it's what you want."

"Not a new residence every year or so," Tracy said with a burst of wry laughter.

"You did grumble about staying with your mother and moving so often. That's why your dad felt you should live with him."

"I know. He thought coming home to the same house every day was security. Maybe it was, but it wasn't enough. I hated being a latchkey kid. I wanted someone at home when I came in the door, or at least someone coming home." She looked at her aunt, and without warning, a lump rose in her throat. She switched on the headlights and peered at the white-and-green street signs high above the freeway while the lump subsided. "Your insisting I come to the chocolate shop after school helped."

"You were watching too much television."

"I remember. I had to exchange a jar of peanut butter, a liter of cola, and a television screen for a cup of hot chocolate and a homework session before I could go outside." The memory of studying amid the clamor of the candy kitchen brought a smile to Tracy's lips.

"Your childhood wasn't all bad," Charli said.

It could have been better, Tracy thought. *I know lots of kids have it worse and don't complain. But if it can be better, I want it better for my children.* She moved her hand from the steering wheel and covered her aunt's hand. "Without you, Aunt Charli, I might weigh four hundred pounds and be a candidate for a circus sideshow or a graduate of the juvenile penal system."

"You exaggerate, but I like to hear that I wasn't an ogre."

"What would you like to eat?" Tracy guided the car toward the right-hand lane.

"Anywhere but the drive-through lane of a fast-food place."

"I'm crushed," Tracy moaned. "I thought you

loved greasy tacos, double-decker hamburgers, and calorie-crowned pizzas.''

''Did you ever hear of too much of a good thing?''

''Gotcha. Seafood and salad.'' She turned toward the off-ramp.

By Wednesday, Tracy knew she had to get away from the shop for lunch. Her shoulders ached from pushing fudge, and she was tempted to see an optometrist about her blurred vision—before she decided the vision problem had little to do with making candy. It was a lack of sleep. She could help the shoulder problem with a lunch break; the sleep problem was a little more difficult.

She ordered a large cola at the snack bar near the hotel and carried it to the walkway bench with a view of the ocean. She kept her gaze away from the hotel, but not her thoughts. She filled her lungs with the salt air and told herself she felt better.

She knew she didn't. How could she feel better when her heart felt like it had a stone tied around it, dragging her down in a pool of despair? She gazed along the path, watching an elderly couple stop to look at the ocean. The silver-haired man slipped his arm around his companion's shoulders and leaned to speak to her. Her laughter was as young as a seventeen-year-old's. Tracy found herself gazing at them with envy. It must be wonderful to have someone to love through the years. Snagging her thoughts in midsentence, she severed them as firmly as a fisherman cutting his line to release a dangerous shark. She exhaled noisily. Of course, it was painful not seeing Clay. *But better a little pain now than a catastrophic attack later,* her mind said logically. She watched the couple move away and picked up the cola cup lethargically. Another couple appeared on the walkway, followed by a lone man. Tracy didn't allow her vision to focus on the walkers. She was here to relax, to forget about the shop—and Clay. To stop seeing Clay in every man on the walkway.

Determinedly, she looked toward the ocean, concentrating on a motorboat skimming over the water beyond the surf. Then she heard his voice and Clay was standing beside the bench, his charismatic smile making the sunlight even brighter.

"Mind if I join you?" Balancing a large paper cup and a fast-food bag, he gestured toward the nearest bench, occupied by three people. "The other 'tables' are full." Without waiting for an answer, he placed his drink on the bench and slid down beside it. "The view is excellent here and I hear the bacon and chicken sandwich is very good."

Tracy couldn't suppress a grin. "I hear the drinks are a little strong."

Clay lifted his paper cup of cola, removed the top, and took a long swallow. "Since it's self-service, I ordered the super size. You may have to walk me home."

Tracy took a minute peeling the wrapper off a plastic straw and pushed it into the slashed opening of her drink. Clay's lighthearted banter slowly relaxed her.

"You want me to be a designated walker?"

"Is that an offer?"

"Dream on. Some of us have to get back to work."

"Work. Where have I heard that word before?"

Noisily, Clay peeled the paper from the sandwich,

releasing the aroma of bacon to mingle with the sea air.

"Work is the one word you are overly familiar with. Speaking of the hotel, if you are eating fast-food take-out, where are your hotel guests seating?"

"The hotel dining rooms, I hope." Clay slid the wrapper aside and bit into the sandwich.

"The water situation has improved."

"Took a lot of midnight work, but we're doing fine. I'm glad it didn't reach Charli's place."

"So is Aunt Charli."

"How's business?"

"Doing so well I may be able to return to Taos sooner than I expected."

He looked at her, the light fading from his eyes. "I thought you were planning to stay six weeks—until Charli's leg is out of the cast."

Tracy had to look away. "I think I should leave as soon as possible."

"Running away?" A trace of bitterness tinged his voice.

"If you want to call it that." Tracy clutched the iced drink, feeling the cold seep through her like an arctic chill. She moved one hand to rest it on her knee, but the cold was still there.

Clay covered her hand with his. "We could work this out. A little compromise on both sides. I'm willing . . ."

The plea stabbed like a knife at Tracy's chest and she interrupted him. "Clay, two weeks more or less won't make any difference in how I feel about you. Nor in how I feel about a workaholic." She looked at him sadly. ''You might change, and then you'd be the unhappy one.'' She pulled her hand away.

''You're not willing to take a chance?''

''It's not only me.''

''There's someone else?''

''I hope there will be. I hope I have two or three children, and I'm thinking about them too.''

''Good heavens, I'm not only battling your ghosts, you drag in future children as well.''

''I thought you liked children.''

''I love children. But for now, I love you. That's enough for me. I hoped it would be enough for you.''

Tracy choked. It would be so easy to give in. To forget her fear that she and Clay would part as her parents had parted. She felt the lump in her throat suffocating her, and when she managed to swallow, it seemed to sink to her chest with even worse complications. She blinked back unshed tears and stared at the sea, watching a graceful white gull swoop toward the surface with dedicated aim until she was sure the tears would not surface. She wanted to think that love could conquer any problem, but she knew she didn't have that kind of trust.

Chapter Ten

Why, Tracy asked herself almost a week later, seated at the work counter and staring into the depths of the satiny dark chocolate as if she might read an answer—why did love not listen to logic? She knew it wasn't logical to love Clay. He represented the disappointments of her childhood, the loneliness, the lack of someone being there. She stirred the melting mixture listlessly. Maybe she had been loved; she'd been told she was loved. Birthday cards from both her parents had been lavish with written avowals of love. But then, they'd been only words with no substance. Or was the proper word sustenance? For words alone hadn't nourished her need for love.

"Tracy." Charli's mild voice brought Tracy back to the present.

Pulling her gaze up from the bowl, Tracy looked inquisitively at her aunt.

168

"Clay was by earlier this morning."

Tracy's hand stilled, letting the creamy chocolate swirl and settle around the wooden spoon as her thoughts became more unsettled.

"New problem at the hotel?" Tracy tried to speak lightly, but the words sounded as heavy to her as if they'd trekked through a chocolate sinkhole.

"Problem? Not that I know of. Remodeling on the east wing of the hotel started yesterday, but he probably counts that a challenge." She grinned. "He invited us to lunch at the hotel. Said it was to celebrate my release from the wheelchair." She rolled her eyes. "I told him graduating to a walking cast didn't mean I'd learned to negotiate well enough to walk to a hotel dining room." Soft laughter rumbled from her throat. "I have a feeling my new cast has nothing to do with the invitation, but I told him I didn't know your schedule for today or if you had any plans. I said one of us would call him."

The murmur of voices at the counter drifted back to fill the quietness, and then the sound stopped with the closing of the front door and silence spread across the kitchen. When the refrigerator motor kicked in, Tracy's hand jerked as if it was on the same current.

Automatically, she resumed stirring to the backdrop of the humming motor. Schedule. So far it included sleeping late again this morning. At Charli's insistence, while Madge drove Charli to the shop. It included shopping at the supermarket and loading the refrigerator with fruit and vegetables and fish and beef. Plans. She planned to drive Aunt Charli home from work and cook a scrumptious dinner. She planned to have lunch with the caterer this week, make mounds of chocolate to fill the display case, and maybe go to Los Angeles on the weekend to see a show with Jolie. She planned to keep herself so busy she wouldn't think of the future. Oh, she had plans, and none of them included lunch with Clay.

She'd spoken to Clay once since the fast-food lunch they'd shared on the bench overlooking the ocean. They'd discussed the coupons for the guest rooms.

She'd taken Charli to the meeting, countering her aunt's argument that the coupons were her idea with a like argument that the business was Charli's. She maneuvered the wheelchair carefully into Clay's office, bending over Charli solicitously to ensure that she was comfortable, thereby giving her own erratic pulse time to settle down. Even leaving had been easier because of Charli. She reversed the routine, avoiding Clay's eyes for fear of encountering the trace of pain she'd seen when she'd first walked into the office.

"Would you be terribly disappointed if we didn't go?" Tracy couldn't look at Charli. "I don't want to leave you with a lot of unfinished work when I go back to Taos next week." She looked up, flustered. "I don't mean . . . I know you've been handling things for years. I just want to help as much as I can. . . . There's lunch with that caterer, and Jolie wants me to visit her in Pasadena and take in a show in L.A. before I leave. . . ."

"Of course not. I can have lunch at the hotel with one of the handsomest men in Costa Corona any day of the week," Charli said in a teasing tone.

Tracy felt her throat tighten and turned away quickly to avoid Charli's observant eyes. Her arm caught the bowl and sent a dark stream of chocolate spinning across the table. The shock loosened the constriction in her neck and she grinned weakly at Charli, embarrassment replacing the sorrow. She was grateful that someone chose that moment to call her aunt to the telephone.

Washing and rinsing the sticky mixture from the counter, she thought of the teasing she'd subjected Clay to for spilling a few drops of chocolate. *Clay, oh, Clay, must everything I do remind me of you?* she mused miserably.

She drove to Pasadena and spent the night with Jolie, driving back on Sunday. She enjoyed the time with Jolie, the light comedy, and the disco, but as soon as she hit the freeway her thoughts returned to Clay.

She arrived in time to help in the store and go to dinner with Charli.

Monday morning started a disastrous week for her, and it hadn't improved by Friday. The ganache burned with her standing over it, the wrong supplies arrived, and she found she'd ordered from a week-old list, and she forgot to have favors ready for a bridal party. However, business improved, and Charli accepted the extra workload without a word and only a trace of weariness. The caterer agreed to purchase his chocolates from Charli. The guest coupons drew customers into the shop, and word-of-mouth advertisement was active. She could return to Taos. She should be happy. But she wasn't. Staying in Costa Corona, so near Clay, kept her confused and miserable.

If only she could change how she felt about his working habits. She couldn't. So it was time to leave.

She was becoming more of a liability to Charli than an asset.

She completed packing one box of the chocolate favors for the computer company banquet, closed the top, and glanced at the white, round face of the clock across from the central work counter. The small hand hovered on five while the longer hand crept toward the half hour. Only a few more hours left of her last Friday in Charli's kitchen. In reality, her last day, since she planned to take the commuter plane to Los Angeles the next day, spend the night with Jolie, and catch a plane to Taos from LAX on Sunday.

She stacked the filled box on a cart and reached for an empty container. With the banquet being held in the Hibiscus Room, she wished she didn't have to deliver the favors. But everyone else was toiling at their own tasks. Anyway, Clay shouldn't be hanging around the service entrance or using the service elevator, she consoled herself.

Filling the last carton, she waved at Charli, tugged the loaded cart out the back door of the shop and into the service door of the hotel. She saw only other workers in jeans or cords or neat white-and-black waiters' uniforms. No one in a three-piece suit and burgundy-and-blue tie, like Clay had worn the last time she'd seen him.

She caught the service elevator, exited, and pushed the cart warily down the hall to the Hibiscus Room. She took a sigh of relief. Safe. She didn't expect to find Clay supervising the room setup.

Pausing inside the doorway, she scanned the room for the banquet captain. A nearby waiter deftly draped a pale persimmon cloth over the circular surface of a large table. A floral centerpiece, silverware, crystal, and blue napkins followed. Tracy's gaze moved on to glance at the other workers erecting tables, placing chairs, arranging water glasses and napkins with a practiced rhythm.

She looked at the dimly lit chandeliers and saw them sparkle as they had the evening she'd met Clay. Could it be only a little over a month ago?

She'd return to visit Charli someday, but she would avoid the main hotel, especially this room. She wondered when the memories would cease to bring an ache to her heart. Would her emotions heal like a broken ankle, allowing her to walk and talk and breathe without thinking of Clay? Maybe away from Costa Corona, away from the sound of the surf and the smell of salt air floating over spring blossoms—and especially away from the chandeliers that turned on lightbulbs in her mind—those memories would fade.

She looked away from the chandeliers and found the woman she sought. The manager crossed to her, scanning each table as she moved.

"Everything here?" The banquet captain barely glanced at the cartons, her attention caught by a tablecloth that drooped dangerously low on one side.

"Except the special chocolates for the speaker's table. I wanted to deliver them separately."

The manager nodded, a scowl appearing briefly on her controlled face. Tracy followed her gaze to see a waiter hurrying through the doorway. He sidestepped tables and workers to make his way to his boss.

"I'm sorry I'm late. I got caught in that traffic tie-up caused by the emergency vehicles. It was even worse because they were headed to the hotel."

Tracy caught her breath. Not another accident in the lobby. She let her breath out carefully, assuring herself it could have nothing to do with the chocolate shop. The fliers that had caused the first chaotic incident had been recycled weeks ago. No line of teenagers had been visible on the walk and the rush of weekend arrivals usually waned by dusk.

The banquet captain's gaze was less inquisitive than Tracy's, but she did give her attention to the waiter.

"Heard it was Mr. Winter." The waiter looked as if he hoped his news would excuse his tardiness.

"Mr. Winter?" Tracy's chest tightened. Had Clay's father had another stroke? A heart attack? She looked at the tardy waiter, but he was already turning away to grasp a table and upright it.

The banquet manager smiled blandly at her and moved away, her eyes scanning the tables as she stopped to speak to a waiter, pointing to the irregular tablecloth. Tracy remained motionless, indecisive. How could she casually catch a commuter flight to L.A. without going to see Clay and express her concern about his father?

She left the busy room, pausing in the hallway to gain a semblance of calm, and took the elevator to Clay's office. It was only a moment's detour, she told herself. She'd have time to return to the shop for the other favors and deliver them well before the banquet guests had finished their second cocktail.

She stopped abruptly in the doorway of the reception room, her gaze jerking from the distraught secretary to an even more distraught white-haired gentleman.

"Mr. Winter?" She was unaware she'd interrupted the secretary.

The secretary paused, turning her head slightly to redirect her gaze across the room. Clement Winter turned with a confused look in his eyes. Tracy was at a loss for words.

Clement Winter didn't look like he'd suffered a stroke or a heart attack or any disabling accident. He was dressed in navy trousers and a light blue jacket, complete with a coordinated pocket handkerchief and tie, as if he was on his way to the lounge for his soda water and lime drink before he went to the dining room.

"There's been an accident." His voice trembled to a stop.

"I heard," Tracy said solicitously. She moved toward Clement. Without warning the waiter's words echoed in her head. Her heart pounded in her chest. Mr. Winter. Clay was also Mr. Winter.

"Where?" It was all she could manage.

Clement nodded back toward the secretary. "Maria said a worker lost his balance descending from the scaffolding with his hands loaded. The foreman and Clay were nearby,"—he took a shuddering breath—"and Clay leaped forward to try to help the man. From what I understand, either the man or the boards fell on Clay." He looked at Maria, as if for confirmation. "Someone used Clay's telephone to call for an ambulance and then they notified Maria so she could have the paramedics directed to the east wing. Maria sent someone to find me."

Tracy nodded, wanting to turn and leave the reception room and race to the scene of the accident. But

Clement had rested his frail hand on her arm as he thanked Maria for calling him.

"I'm going to the east wing," he added. He dropped his hand and started past Tracy.

Maria reached a hand forward as if to stop the elderly man, then drew back and carefully balanced the tips of her fingers on the desktop. "The paramedic team may have taken Clay to the ambulance by now, Mr. Winter." Her voice grew calmer as she spoke. "Let me call the front desk and see if they've passed through the lobby."

Clement hesitated reluctantly, and Tracy waited beside him with even less patience, until Maria made the call.

"The ambulance crew is going through the lobby now. Carol"—she paused—"Carol works in admissions. . . . She said they're transporting someone on a gurney and trying to support another 'walking wounded.' "

Maria looked at Clement with concern. "If you want to go to the hospital, I'll call someone to drive you."

Tracy spoke the words without hesitation. "I'll drive you, Mr. Winter." The words were in the air before she could stop them. With the damage already done, she waved at Maria and preceded Clement out the door, telling herself she was going to the hospital for Clement's sake. But it was all she could do to follow his slow, unsteady pace to the elevator.

Tracy circled the hospital, parking in a lot near the emergency room entrance. Remembering Clay's patience with his father in his slow progress through the hotel lobby that spring morning so long ago, Tracy strove to imitate it. With adrenaline pumping through her body, it wasn't easy to separate her feet and plead with them to pretend they were encased in weighted sandals.

The young receptionist was calm and noninformative until she learned the inquirer was related to the patient in the nearby room. She turned to Clement and smiled attentively when Tracy introduced him as Clay's father. Tracy was impressed, not caring if the respect was due to his age or his reputation as having once owned the well-known hotel.

The young woman walked around the counter separating them and motioned to a doorway. "If you'll wait in this area," she said, indicating the room beyond an open doorway, "the doctor or a nurse will come and talk to you after your son has been examined."

Waiting until Clement was seated, Tracy sank on a chair nearby, reached automatically for a magazine from the table next to her chair, and scanned it absently. The contents listed inside were vaguely familiar. Dully, she flipped to the cover and scanned the date. Her lips pursed. Two years old. She closed the magazine, realizing that in her present mood she would call a sneeze an outbreak of pneumonia or an outdated magazine a lack of professional upkeep.

She glanced at Clement, trying to forestall the thought that Clay's presence in the construction area was unnecessary. He had weekly—or knowing Clay, daily—conversations with the construction superintendent regarding the east wing. But knowing Clay, although he could pick up his telephone to inquire about the progress of the east wing, she doubted if it was unusual for him to leave his office and see the work himself.

She picked up the daily newspaper, reading the large print above the articles. The U.S. Centers for Disease Control had another study to report on accidents. She turned to the next page, glancing at Clement, wondering if the hospital supplied decaf coffee to anxiety-ridden relatives. Or anxiety-ridden non-relatives! Restlessly, she flipped back to the article. "Seventeen killed daily, CDC claims." Construction workers, she noted, rated high on the percentage list, but the article didn't list managerial personnel. They were supposed to be in their comfortable, safe offices, waiting for a heart attack, Tracy thought. She looked up to see another worried friend or relative enter the room with a Styrofoam cup.

"Coffee?" Tracy inquired, feeling no embarrassment speaking to a stranger who shared the anxiety in the room.

"Coffee machine down the hall to the right," the young man said, not looking at her.

Tracy stood, asked if Clement would like coffee and, when he nodded, walked to the coffee machine.

Returning, she sipped the hot, strong liquid and tried to close her mind to the thought of Clay's injuries. Worrying wouldn't make them any less. It would help, though, if someone told her and Clement the seriousness of the wounds, she mused.

One thing the accident showed was that she didn't have to wait for a heart attack to claim Clay. Common accidents were everywhere. With Clay's intent interest in everything around him, he was bound to find one.

She looked at Clement, seeing his head bowed, his

unfocused eyes on the floor. "I know you're worried." She placed her cup on the table. "Maybe I can find a nurse and see if the doctor has examined Clay."

Clement looked up, his eyes focusing. "I'm all right." He took an audible breath. "This isn't the first time I've waited in this room to hear about Clay. Though he was much younger then. The summers he spent with me weren't dull. If a surfer was in distress in shark-infested waters, Clay was the one to swim out to help." He grinned weakly. "I learned to accept it long ago."

Accept. The word echoed in Tracy's mind, and she stared at Clement, remembering Clay had uttered it the first time in reference to his attitude to his father's lifestyle. Clay had said love was acceptance. Maybe it was. The love between Clay and Clement was evident.

She knew she loved Clay. No doubt about that. So why wasn't it easy for her to accept Clay as he was and trust him to adjust his working hours to include a family?

She lifted the cup, tasting liquid as cold and bitter as her thoughts. She wasn't sure she could accept him as he was—accept him without nagging. Then there would be the arguments and the heartache and the separation and the loneliness. The risk was too great.

She was on her feet at the sound of footsteps in the hall and met the nurse at the door.

"I'm sorry I didn't get back to you sooner. Another accident, so we are backed up a little." She walked inside the room, speaking to Clement. "Your son will be out shortly. The doctor is putting the finishing touches to his cast."

"Cast?"

"I didn't tell you his forearm is broken? Compound fracture. Beyond that, a few bruises." Her smile was as brief as her stay. She swept past Tracy with a nod.

Tracy felt her knees wobble and thought how silly it was to feel weak now. Clay was all right. She could continue with whatever she'd been doing—could leave for Los Angeles tomorrow and Taos the next day.

Then Clay walked to the door of the waiting room wearing a sling and his usual charismatic smile, and her plans to catch the plane took off without her.

"I heard there was someone in here who'd give me a ride back to the hotel."

Tracy didn't move, not sure her knees were stable yet. "Shouldn't you go home and rest?"

"Dad has to go to the hotel."

"Then you can drive him home," Clement said cheerfully. "Maybe he'll let you tuck him in. I'm sure he wouldn't let me."

Only when Tracy drove down the circular drive did she remember the rest of the favors for the convention dinner. She doubted if anyone in the shop had noticed. Charli should have left with Madge, who was dropping her off at Rose's for dinner. She looked back toward the shop, trying to see if the lights were still on while she said good night to Clement. She couldn't tell.

She looked back at Clay, reluctant to have him leave. "I can drive you home after I see if the rest of an order was delivered to the Hibiscus Room. If I'm not too late. The cocktail hour should be over and the dinner guests seated and the banquet hostess fuming if the favors aren't on the head table.''

''My accident have something to do with this?''

''Why would you think that?''

''You were worried about me?''

''I was concerned about Clement.''

''I'll let you drive me home if you'll let me go with you. Not that I can be much help.'' Clay opened the car door. ''You can leave the car here and call the shop from the desk,'' he suggested. ''Save walking down there.''

He walked around the car and spoke to the doorman.

Lindon answered on the first ring, saying the hostess had just called and he was on his way to deliver the favors.

Tracy relayed the words to Clay. ''I should go up and apologize. I don't want to leave Aunt Charli with any problems.''

''Where you go this evening, I'll go,'' Clay teased. ''I'm too weak to stay in the lobby by myself.''

''Then you should be too weak to go upstairs,'' Tracy countered. But she was thrilled to have him near.

The banquet captain accepted her apologies, giving her attention more to Clay and expressing concern about his injuries before turning back to her duties.

Tracy looked across the room at the glass doors, and as if Clay could read her thoughts, he slipped his hand under her elbow and directed her toward the terrace. ''We can leave by the terrace if you don't mind the stairs.''

Tracy thought she wouldn't mind six flights of stairs if it kept Clay beside her longer.

They moved through the doorway, closing the glass behind them, and walked to the banister.

With the doors closed, the room behind them receded and they stood on a small concrete island enclosed in a bower of scarlet flowers and lush greenery. Bougainvillea blossoms clung to the climbing plant, dipping and dancing in the sea breeze. The ficus plant waved lazily. Beyond the courtyard and the beaches, a rising moon glowed on the water, highlighting the churning wake of a returning boat.

Clay walked around her, slipping his right arm around her waist to pull her against his body. "Do you really want to leave all this?"

Tracy tried to hear only the teasing in his voice, but the pain was there. "It isn't easy."

"It isn't necessary."

Tracy was silent.

"Tracy, I can't promise to be home at six o'clock every day, or have every weekend free, but I'm willing to try. Try very hard. Couldn't you meet me half-way?"

Tracy turned, slipping in his arm to face him, and tilted her head to gaze into his hazel eyes. She was unable to recall the reasons she'd thought were etched in stone.

"I should go to Taos and get my things and resign from my job. I don't suppose you could come with me."

"You suppose wrong. Do I have time to pack a toothbrush or shall I buy one at the airport shop?"

"I'm not leaving tonight."

He sagged against her briefly. "That's good. I don't know if I could stay up as far as the airport, let alone Taos."

Guilt assailed Tracy. "I should have taken you home right away. Are you in much pain?"

"The nurse gave me a couple of pills. That could be why I feel so tired."

"I'll take you home now."

"I like that. You can tuck me in." He pulled her closer, groaning at the cast between them. His head lowered, his lips touching hers in a kiss that sent spirals of warmth radiating from her head to her toes.

Tracy clung to him, conscious of the injured arm even as she absorbed the touch of his lips.

He lifted his head and looked into her eyes. "Do you believe in long engagements?"

"Engagement?" She grinned at him impishly. "I thought we'd just broached the courting part."

"Do you believe in long courtships?" Clay trailed kisses along her cheek.

Tracy moaned softly. The smile in her heart bubbled upward, spreading to her lips and her eyes. "No longer than necessary." She stepped back. "I think it's time I took you home to start recuperating so you can begin courting."

She turned toward the stairs, but before she could take a step he moved forward. Her back met his chest as he dipped his head to kiss her ear. She sighed, gazing at the distant ocean. "Nice place to begin a courtship. Lovely view, with the moonlight on the water and the banana leaves swaying in the breeze."

"Our publicity department could use you." He placed another kiss on her ear.

"You would think of that," Tracy teased. But she found she didn't mind.

"I can't forget about business if I'm going to take on the responsibility of marriage. I have to keep a roof over our heads."

"You're rushing the courtship."

"Just letting you know my intentions." His ar circled her waist.

Tracy nestled in his arm, the doubts of the past crumbling. She meant to see that they were away like the ruins of a destroyed building. Their future, hers and Clay's, would rise on a new foundation of trust. She'd meet him more than halfway.

She breathed contentedly. Even though her Prince Charming rode the elevator instead of climbing a trellis to the balcony, it didn't make being here with him any less romantic.

"I like your intentions." She relaxed her shoulders, gathering warmth from his nearness. She'd teach him to play and he'd teach her to work. They might have it perfect in twenty or thirty years.

It would be time well spent. She knew now there could be no happiness for her without Clay.